The Half Days

An ex-pat adventure

In Southern Italy

Sedley Proctor

This book is entirely a work of fiction. The names, characters and incidents portrayed in it are the work of the author's imagination. Any resemblance to actual persons, living or dead, events or locations is entirely coincidental, but completely plausible.

The Half Days
First published in Great Britain by
Leopard Publishing Ventures Ltd
Hampshire SO212PR
www.the half days.com

Copyright © 2015 Sedley Proctor

Sedley Proctor asserts the moral right to be identified as the author of this work.

ISBN: 978-0-9574550-2-3

For my Apulian friends who continue to bask in the sun.

CONTENTS

The Jollies

The trattoria was a small family affair, tucked away in the shade of a narrow lane in the old Jewish quarter. I sat down at a table on the pavement and ordered pasta with clams. The padrone brought me a carafe of white wine. For the second course I ordered *frittura*, little baby octopus fried in batter. Afterwards he brought me a lemon sorbet, followed by coffee and a grappa.

"*Inglese*," he said.

I nodded.

I continued to nod, as he began to chat away. In the end he brought out a pack of cards. It was a Neapolitan deck.

"*Giochi?*" he said. "Do you play?"

He began to explain the rules, spreading out the *denari*, the money cards before me.

"These," he said, "are the jollies, the jokers in the pack."

I nodded; he dealt two hands.

The padrone kept dealing, and I kept drinking his grappa and nodding.

After a while, it was clear I would keep losing my jollies. I asked the padrone for the bill.

The padrone stuck up his fingers.

One was missing.

"*Nove*," I said. "Nine."

"Well," he said, "you can't play cards. At least, you know how to count."

It was four o'clock in the afternoon. I had lost track of time.

If that episode sticks in my mind, I like to think of it as the first of those half days stretching into the summer nights where the business of the day was forgotten in a round of carnival pleasures.

I frutti proibiti sono sempre i piu dolci.
Forbidden fruit is always sweetest. - Italian proverb

***

Forbidden Fruit

Julia was touched.

By chance they had found out that it was her birthday. Patrizia's cousins and friends arrived. The chairs had been pushed aside and the tables laid out as a buffet with an abundance of Southern Italian fare: *arancini, pizza rustica* and *pasta al forno* made by Patrizia's aunt, and a huge bowl of *crudiaola* pasta with cherry tomatoes, dressed with *ricotta mazzotica* and basil. Everyone had brought her a present - something they deemed might be useful for her new life, including a set of sheets and a tablecloth.

In the morning Patrizia and her cousin, Pierliugi bundled all her worldly possessions including what remained of the *pasta al forno* and the birthday cake into the car and they drove the fifty kilometres to her new home.

The two friends embraced.

"I hope you find what you are looking for," said Patrizia. "*In bocca al lupo!*"

"*Crepi,*" said Julia.

"Come and visit me in Milan."

It was her first day in town. Julia got up late, and, as it was a sunny day, she decided to go to the beach. She found a salumeria in the row of shops around the corner from the flat, and got them to make her a panino with mozzarella and San Daniele. From a one thousand lira shop she also bought a beach mat and some sun cream. Then she walked along the sea front, up past the solitary fishermen and people bathing on the rocks, to the local beach, which was known as Pane e Pomodoro, or Bread and Tomatoes.

Julia sat on the beach all afternoon, reading a book and idly playing with the sand. From time to time she dipped her toes in the water. Once and only once she went for a swim out towards the rocks that acted as a kind of breakwater in the artificial bay of the beach. As the sun went down, she dried off and packed up her things and went home.

When she reached the square, she stopped off in the bar under the flat and ordered a lemon *granita*.

A fisherman stood on the side of the road with a bucket at his feet. He wore yellow gumboots and overalls. Like an ancient shellback or servant of Neptune. Old men sat out in the square in their shirt sleeves and swallows flew around the gable of the old Scuola Elementare.

The charm and warmth of the scene tingled through her body.

"*Ti piace la granita,*" the barman said.

Julia turned back to the barman.

"*È buonissima,*" she said.

The barman smiled. "I've got a piece of land out in the country," he said. "I grow the lemons myself. I've got figs and cherries, too," he said. "The figs are still in season."

He paused as he wiped one of his cups and placed it on the shelf behind him.

"Do you like figs?"

"I like your lemon granita."

The barman chuckled. "Next time you must try my fig ice cream."

Julia fell asleep in her bikini. When she woke up, it was the middle of the night. She stepped out onto the little balcony overlooking the square to smoke a cigarette. Her half-naked body tingled in the warm night air. As she climbed back into bed, she had the feeling of being at home in a way she could not remember.

The following day, she went back to the beach. Although the sun was out, only dedicated sun worshippers were about, one of whom sat, cross-legged, holding a mirror under his chin in a bid, she thought, to catch the last rays of the summer as joggers and cyclists sweated on the path.

Julia dozed off. When she woke up, the sun was back out. She turned and lay on her front.

"Ciao, bella."

A coffee brown African with a wide-brimmed hat smiled down at her, showing all his ivory teeth.

"On holiday? *Turista?*"

"Teacher."

"*Insegnante, parli italiano?*"

"*Un po.*"

"*Je suis Daniel.*"

"*Salud, Daniel.*"

"*Tu, come ti chiami?*"

"*Je m'appelle Julie.*"

Between their French and Italian his eyes flitted over her body.

"*Che fai?*" he said.

"Just hanging here. And you?"

She used the Italian word *cazzeggiare*.

"Me, too. I also sell things."

"Well," she said, hitching up her bikini top, "what are you going to sell me?"

Daniel pulled a selection of dresses from his bag and spread them out on Julia's beach mat.

Julia put one of the dresses on over her bikini.

"What do you think?"

"It looks nice on you. *Sei carina.*"

Daniel pulled out a little mirror from his bag.

Julia peered at herself.

The neckline of the dress was decorated with little flowers.

"*Mi piaccono i fiori*," she said. "I'll take it."

Daniel came to pick her up in a battered old Granada. He had brought along a friend. His name was Cofi. He was slight of build and wore a pair of horn-rimmed spectacles.

"*Prego*," he said, stepping out of the car and opening the door at the back.

Julia wanted to laugh at his serious, professorial expression, but stopped herself just in time.

They drove up past the beach and along the sea front for a few kilometres before turning down a narrow lane. The lane twisted and turned round increasingly narrow bends; they pulled up at a shabby looking villa surrounded by bamboo plants and prickly pears.

They parked the car outside the gate and walked up the drive. They did not go in the house but climbed the stairs to the roof where a barbecue was under way.

There was already a fair crowd, sitting on garden chairs and old sofas or standing around drinking and eating snacks off plastic plates around a long table with party food. There was a smaller table with a stereo, but no one was listening to it. Instead the throng was gathered round two student types with guitars. They were singing old, Italian hits from the seventies and eighties. People drifted in and out of the throng with their barbecue food.

Daniel got a plastic plate and piled some sausages off the barbecue onto it. Julia had found some forks, and they sat sharing the sausages from the plate and drinking the beers they had brought in a plastic bag.

After a while, the musicians stopped playing; someone put Almamagretta on the stereo and everyone got up to dance.

Julia began to sway to the music on her own until she noticed Cofi at her shoulder.

"Are you enjoying the party?"

Cofi smiled.

"And you?"

The party fizzled out some time in the middle of the night to the sad strains of Neapolitan dub.

Daniel and Cofi took Julia back to her flat. "*Zitti!*" she said, giggling as they walked in through the door. "We mustn't wake my flat mates."

"Not a whisper," said Daniel.

"As quiet as mice," Cofi said, grinning.

Julia need not have worried; the two Africans were as good as gold. She woke up on the sofa with a blanket over her. They had made coffee and bought some cornetti.

"Nutella," she exclaimed, as Cofi put the cornetti on the table. The chocolate was oozing out of them. "I haven't had nutella since I was a child."

After breakfast, they went for a drive along the sea front to San Giorgio. Here they found a spot at the side of the road and sat on the rocks sunning themselves.

Julia rolled up her jeans and paddled around in the shallows. Following suit, Cofi slipped on one of the rocks and fell in.

Daniel cracked up. "What are you playing at, man?"

If Cofi looked annoyed, he did not say anything.

Julia wanted to laugh, too, but she didn't because he looked crossly at Daniel.

"I let you into a secret," said Daniel. "Cofi cannot swim."

This was how it began, her flirtation with the so-called *marocchini*, the Senegalese street-sellers. For one delicious moment Julia thought she might succumb to temptation before pulling herself up and casting aside the dangerous nonsense running through her head when Cofi caught her and pulled her to him in the water.

"Cofi," she said, "what are you doing?"

"What does it look like?" he said.

"I don't know what it looks like," she said, "let's not think about it too much."

He laughed.

"You are right," he said. "Daniel always says I think far too much."

Julia's contract at the British School began the following day. She was busy getting to know the school and the other members of staff. She did not see Cofi until a few days later, when she bumped into him in the square under the flat wheeling his trolley.

"*Bella*," he said, beaming. "*Come stai?*"

"Did you have any luck?"

"The beach season is over," he said with a shrug.

"You didn't sell any dresses."

"I didn't sell anything."

"Not a thing."

"I got chased by a dog."

"*Che sfiga*! How unlucky!"

Cofi shrugged.

Julia was amused by his diffidence.

"Daniel always says I am like a marabout."

"What does that mean?"

"I think what he means, although I do not agree, is that I live on air."

"Signorina, you have come for your lemon granita… What about the fig ice cream?"

Cofi stared at the barman.

Ignoring Cofi, the barman turned to Julia and winked:

"*I frutti proibiti sono sempre i piu dolci.*"

If she knew what it meant, Julia chose to ignore it and finished her drink.

Cofi had already gone outside.

She followed him onto the street. They walked down to the sea front and sat on one of the benches where they looked across at the harbour wall with its green-capped lighthouse.

"Are you angry?"

Cofi shrugged.

She took his hand. He pulled it away.

"Is that what I am? Forbidden fruit."

"That makes two of us," she said.

Cofi smiled.

Julia lived another nine months in the flat above the bar, but she never went back there for the lemon *granita*. She had a stubborn streak and would not give up on the forbidden fruit.

The Basket

In the first block of flats where I lived for two months while everything else was arranged or, as they like to put it here, *sistemato*, was a wonderful old gated lift. The lift had wooden panelling and glass windows decorated with deco motifs. At the back of the lift there was even a little red upholstered seat where you could prop your shopping or rest your feet. It was always such a stately progress in that lift, one felt like a dowager duchess or a queen ascending to the top.

In Katarina's flats, however, there was no lift. As we lived on the top floor, it was a terrible sweat to get in the shopping, especially if you were lugging up bottles of Monticchio water; which is why I feel it's important to mention the Professoressa's basket.

The Professoressa lived on the third floor, and her basket was attached to a pulley. She had an arrangement with the fellow from the salumeria next door. The Professoressa would send down her basket. "*A post,*" he would shout from down below when all the bottles of Monticchio water were in. "*A post*," she would shout back when the bottles had arrived safely at her floor.

It was such an elegant solution, or so I thought until, one day, I saw the fellow from the salumeria lugging the bottles of Monticchio up the stairs.

"*Buongiorno,* Professore," he said, after pausing for breath.

"*Buongiorno,*" I said. "What's going on?"

"*Piccoli diavoli,*" he said. "Those kids of the plumber are little devils."

"What have they done?"

"*Hanno meso degli scarafaghi dentro la borsa della professoressa,*" he said. "They put some cockroaches in the professoressa's shopping."

"How terrible," I said, though I could not help giggling all the way down the street until I reached the faculty and spat it out to Gavin.

Mrs. Wilson's Necklace

The impresario, Tony di Curtis was sitting in his office with a cigar in his hand when he turned to Katarina and anyone else who cared to listen to him (since the door was half open and an act was pacing outside) trumpeting his desire to learn English from a real Englishman.

"By the way," he said. "I don't want one of those Italian teachers who have lived five years in the Bronx. I want the real thing, I want *madre lingua*."

His tongue rolled around the word as if indeed it was the clue to his ambition.

"In that case," said Katarina, "You better have Patrick."

Tony raised his eyebrow.

"How can an Irishman be mother tongue?"

"He works at the English faculty."

"Well, does that qualify him as mother tongue?"

"Tony, he is mother tongue Irish. Besides, he is the best. Everyone says it."

"Like who?"

"Ask around if you want. Honestly I don't know why you bothered to ask me if you can't accept my suggestions."

"*Va bene*," he said, "have you got his number?"

"You want me to phone him now. Or are you going to deal with this contract?"

"Later will do. Anyway," said Tony, slowly adjusting to the idea as he puffed on his cigar, "I always preferred the Irish to the English. They make much better whisky."

"*Ignorante*," she said, "the English don't make whisky."

"What do you mean?"

"Even I know whisky is Scottish."

Di Curtis shrugged. "It's the same thing, isn't it?"

"And another thing," said Katarina, "he wants the lesson at eight o'clock in the morning."

"Well," said Patrick. "Nothing ever happens in the faculty before ten."

"Don't think for a minute he'll be an easy student."

"Don't you worry, Katy. He'll get used to my ways."

"All the same," said Katarina. "I better keep an eye on him."

As good as her word, Katarina entered Tony's office on the morning of the first lesson.

"What do you want?"

"Don't you want your money?"

"You counted it?"

"You know I did, Tony."

"Put it away in the safe."

"Then I need the keys."

Tony opened the desk drawer and threw the keys on the table.

"Stai attento. La gente è forba," he said, turning to Patrick. "How do you say that in English?"

"Beware. People are cunning."

Tony looked at Katarina and repeated the phrase. "Beware. People are cunning."

"What about you, Tony?" said Katarina, who did not like Tony to get away with such pronouncements. "Are you cunning, too?"

"What about it?" said Di Curtis, who, in spite of his ambitions, was from a small town in the middle of nowhere. "Where I grew up, in contrast to this den of thieves I have the misfortune to live in is scrupulously honest."

"In that case," said Katarina, "you won't mind if you give me last week's wages."

"What, are you suggesting I am tight?" Tony bristled.

"I wasn't suggesting anything of the sort," said Katarina, winking at Patrick over his shoulder. "By the way," she said, putting three notes on the table, "here is the money for Patrick's lesson."

"What did I say, Patrick? *La gente è sempre forba.*"

"Remember, Patrick. Don't let him get away with anything. You must test him every day on his irregular verbs."

"Go. What's the past of go?"

"Went."

"That's right. Go, went, gone. Even I remember that. Now," Tony said, turning to Katarina, "get off with you and let me get on with my lesson."

As it turned out Tony and Patrick got along like a house on fire. Tony would invite Patrick to the club of which he was proprietor, known in its current manifestation as the Gorgeous. Patrick would profess to be thoroughly entertained by the harlequinade parading through the Gorgeous, even the tired old variety acts and Beatles cover bands. The lessons went on all through the winter and into the spring. Sometimes Tony was in Milan and sometimes he was in Rome. Patrick did not mind very much. Things were beginning to hot up in the faculty; exams were just round the corner, and, besides, his mother was coming over from Dublin.

"Katy, I can't thank you enough. It is very kind of you to agree to put Mother up."

"Don't mention it," said Katarina. "We're looking forward to it."

"I promise she is a very easy guest. She'll cook us a stew and is not averse to doing a bit of ironing. Mind you," said Patrick, "I don't know how she is going to occupy herself while I am stuck in the exam hall. I will hardly be able to take her to the beach."

Katarina smiled. If she was aware of a ruse, she chose to ignore it.

"Never you mind, Patrick," she said. "I am sure one of us will be able to take her to the beach. Besides, Tony owes me a day off."

"Katy, you angel!" said Patrick. "I don't know what I would do without you."

San Vito was an old sixteenth century monastery that overlooked a rugged bay with a beach tower where Katarina liked to spread herself out upon the rocks. If here there was no sand to speak of, she knew of a nice spot a little further along the beach road. "You'll love it, Mrs. Wilson," she said. "Everyone does when they see it."

"Katy," said Mrs. Wilson, "I cannot imagine anything more heavenly."

A path cut between whitewashed villas onto a small sandy beach. At the height of summer the beach heaved with chubby mothers and their little charges, gangs of teenage boys horsing around between the parasols and cold boxes and the sultry Lolitas and their supersize girlfriends, but the season was still a few weeks off. There was no one on the beach, just an old couple looking after their young grandchild.

There was not a ripple on the water when Katarina swam out into the little bay and hauled herself up on a green bank of rock. It provided a perfect platform from which to dive into the water and follow the little fish as they nibbled at the seaweed.

Returning from her swim, she found Mrs. Wilson ensconced with the old couple. They all laughed as the little boy filled his swimming trunks with pebbles and sand.

"Isn't that priceless!" said Mrs. Wilson.

"*È troppo ridiculo*," she said.

Katarina lay back and slipped into a pleasant daydream that may have taken in the little boy and the holiday villa over yonder when she received a call from her sister.

"What is it, *mia sorella?*"

"Don't hold your breath," she said. "*È stato un furto a casa.*"

On the surface Katarina may have appeared quite cool and collected, but Mrs. Wilson was not to be fooled as she pulled the towel out from under her feet and began to beat out the sand.

"What on earth is the matter, Katy?"

"There's been a burglary," she said.

"Oh, what a nuisance," said Mrs. Wilson, "I thought things like that only happened back home."

"Have they taken anything?"

"I don't think so. After all, what was there to take?"

Although nothing seemed very much out of place; there was the usual pile of books and papers on the dining room table; the contents of Mrs. Wilson's suitcase were in a pile on the bed.

"How did they get in?" said Katarina, turning to her sister.

"Over the roof."

"The window was open."

"I thought I shut it before I went out."

"We really must do something about that window."

"Do you think the Vicino was involved?"

Amelia shrugged.

"He's never done anything to us before."

"Oh, no," said Mrs. Wilson suddenly. "I was sure I left it in here…"

"Mrs. Wilson, you are red."

"Am I, Katy? I don't feel very flushed at the moment. I can't find my necklace. I was sure I put it here in the bottom of this shoe bag."

"What's the Signora saying?"

"She can't find her necklace. She thinks it's been stolen."

"What does she expect? She walks around dressed like that? She sticks out a mile."

"You're quite right. It's idiotic."

"Well," said Mrs. Wilson who was listening to all this without understanding a word. "Are we going to call the police?"

"Oh, Mrs. Wilson," Katarina said. "I don't think you understand. The people here are all thieves."

"Are you talking about the Police?" said Mrs. Wilson.

"No, Mrs. Wilson, I am talking about our neighbours."

"She's right," said Amelia after a pause. "Perhaps we should call the police."

"What if the Vicino is involved?"

Amelia shrugged.

"He's never done anything to us before. Why should he start now?"

"Even still, I think we shouldn't discount it."

In the middle of all this Patrick walked in through the door.

"What's going on?" he said. "I thought you were at the beach."

"Patrick," said Mrs. Wilson. "Thieves have been here. They've stolen my necklace."

"Oh, Mother, I am sorry. Which necklace was that? Not Aunt Delia's?"

"No, not that one. The other one."

"You mean the one that boy before dad gave you on the ship."

"Yes, that one."

"Are you okay, Mother?"

"Of course, I am okay, Patrick. It's the girls I'm worried about. There's nothing worse than someone coming into your home and going through your things."

"Your mother isn't upset? - She's putting a brave face on it."

"Well," said Patrick. "she had that necklace a long time. It had sentimental value."

"Of course, there might be a way of getting it back," said Katarina. "We could go and talk to the Vicino."

Patrick looked bemused. "I thought you were always joking about the Vicino."

"It's no joke," said Amelia. "He has been in prison."

"All the same don't you think we ought to call the police?"

Katarina shrugged.

"What can they do?"

"How about investigate the scene of the crime."

"It's not that simple, Patrick," said Amelia.

"Well, it can't be that difficult. All you have to do is swab for fingerprints. To the best of my knowledge this has been common practice in police forces for well over a century."

"Oh, I don't know," said Katarina, suddenly throwing up her arms and feeling thoroughly deflated. "I need to go to the bathroom."

Katarina shut herself in the bathroom and sat down on the toilet. Just as she weighing up the options between the Vicino and the police, she saw it on the shelf above the basin, beside the cup with the toothbrushes. The necklace belonged to neither her sister nor herself; it was far too expensive looking for that.

Mrs. Wilson was over the moon. "Katy," she said, "how stupid of me!"

"There you go, Mother," said Patrick. "We are lucky we didn't have to call the police."

"I am sure," she said. "Though I can't see what's wrong with calling the police."

"Never mind, Mother. Just be thankful you got your necklace back. The question is what are we going to do with it now?"

"I've got it," said Katarina suddenly.

"What?"

"Tony's safe."

"What about Tony's safe?"

Katarina looked at her sister and smiled.

"Never you mind, *mia sorella*! Why don't you go and do something useful like put on the pasta?"

"Why do I always have to cook?"

"Isn't it obvious?" said Katarina. "You're a much better cook than me."

A few days later, Tony di Curtis was sitting in his office contemplating the cigar butt that smoldered in the ashtray on his desk when Katarina burst in on his thoughts.

"Tony," she said. "What have you done with the necklace?"

"What necklace?"

"The one I put in your safe."

Tony looked embarrassed.

"If you must know," he said. "I gave it to my wife."

"Why did you do that?"

"Well, don't look at me like that. I thought someone had left it in the club."

"Tony, you idiot," she said. "That necklace belongs to Mrs. Wilson, Patrick's mother. She's going home tomorrow."

"I can't ask for it back now," he said. "My wife will think I have a mistress. Anyway, what were you doing putting her necklace in the safe?"

"I told you! I put it there for safe keeping."

"Well, I don't remember."

"That's what you always say."

"Is it my fault if you put other people's necklaces in my safe?"

"The question is," said Katarina, "how are you going to make it up to me and Patrick?"

Tony shrugged.

"I could always buy you another necklace."

Patrick was super busy. In fact, he had been busy for quite a while, though it always was the case just prior to Christmas when he received the phone call from his mother.

"Patrick," she said, "you are going to think I am an absolute fool, but I cannot for the life of me remember what I did with my necklace."

Now you might think as Tony might say Mrs. Wilson was either extremely cunning or *forba*. If she had forgotten she had made Katarina a present of the necklace, Patrick was and always would be a confirmed bachelor.

Mummy's Boy

Dario was the eternal student; at thirty-five he still lived at home. Officially he was at work on his thesis which was rather grandly entitled "Upon Nationalization and the post-war Italian economy" but, if truth were known, he wasn't doing anything very much except hanging out with Gavin.

When Gavin went to the Maltese, Dario always turned up. When Gavin was off to a party, Dario would tag along. When Gavin was going to a gig in Rome, he would always find Dario among the audience. Dario was what the locals call *piccicoso*, or sticky. He stuck to you, like the pads of a fly on a hot summer's day.

One day, Gavin got so fed up with him he told him where to go.

They happened to be sitting in Gavin's flat; Dario was stretched on Gavin's sofa with a joint rolled by Gavin.

On the coffee table was a pair of sunglasses belonging to Gavin. Dario picked up the sunglasses and threw them across the room. Retrieving the sunglasses, he crushed them under foot. "Shithead," he said; then he stormed out of the flat.

Gavin did not hear anything from Dario after that.

About a year later, they met, by chance, on the seafront.

Dario was with a girl whose name was Cecilia. He seemed pleased to see Gavin.

"Shithead."

"Mummy's Boy. You still haven't paid for my sunglasses."

"Fuck you."

Dario came back into Gavin's life. When Gavin went out, Dario would still tag along, but it wasn't quite the same because Dario had finished his degree and was going to get married to Cecilia.

Dario asked Gavin if he would give a speech in English. "No one will understand," he said, "except you, me and Cecilia."

"I'll do it," said Gavin, "on the condition I get to slag you off."

"Shithead," said Dario.

"Mummy's Boy."

There is no bombast, no similes, flowers, digressions, or unnecessary descriptions. Everything tends towards catastrophe. - Castle of Otranto, H. Walpole

***

Eight Hundred and Thirteen Martyrs

"Here in the south, as I am sure you know," said the priest, who was a little, pink-faced gnome of a man with thick-rimmed glasses, "we have an expression:

Mamma li turchi!

One tells it to little children to get them to behave. But to our way of thinking the Turk is not just a bogeyman, but a historical enemy."

It was the middle of the afternoon, and it was very cool in the priest's church. If I was not yet cool, however, I realized I was in for one of those long explanations that would eventually catch up with my repose in his temple of cool.

"The year was 1480 and the date was the 28 July when the Pasha launched an attack on our town. He brought his ships up to the port and landed beneath the walls of the city. The garrison was unable to resist the bombardment for long, and abandoned the main part of the city on the following day. They retreated, along with the townsfolk, into the citadel whilst the Turks began bombarding the neighboring houses.

The Pasha's terms were ostensibly generous. "If you surrender," he told them, "you will forfeit the town but I will let you to live."

"The Christian's response to the Pasha's demands was firm. "*Non arrendiamci*," they said. "We will not surrender to an infidel."

When a second messenger was sent to the walls to repeat the demands, he was met with arrows from the walls. To settle the issue, the leaders of the castle defense climbed to the top of the tower and threw the keys of the city into the sea. "*Venite a trovarci se osate!* Come and get us if you dare!"

After a fifteen-day siege, the Pasha ordered the final assault. His soldiers broke through the defenses and captured the citadel. When the walls were breached, the

Turks fought their way through the town. Upon reaching the cathedral they found the Archbishop, fully vested and crucifix in hand, awaiting them. "Who dares enter the house of God with swords drawn?"

"Abjure the Christian faith," said the Pasha's men, taunting the archbishop. "Throw away your crucifix and embrace Islam."

"I cannot renounce my faith any more than deny the truth of Christ's suffering," said the archbishop. "For the name of Jesus and the protection of the Church, I am ready to embrace death."

The Turks showed no mercy. The archbishop's head was cut off before his weeping congregation. Here the chronicler relates that the crown of his head was separated from the head in such a way that blood, white with the brain, and the brain no less red from the blood dyed the floor of the cathedral."

If I chose to express my shock, the priest did not appear to notice.

Ignoring me, he went on:

"The archbishop's two companions, the bishop and the count were to meet a similar fate. "Abjure the

Christian faith," said the Pasha's men. "Throw down your crucifixes and embrace Islam."

When they refused, their bodies were slowly sawn in half. As was the custom, all the priests were murdered and the cathedral was stripped of its symbols and turned into a stable for horses.

After desecrating the Cathedral, the Turks gathered the women and older children to be sold into slavery. Here the chronicler relates another atrocity. Men over fifteen years old, small children, and infants were slain.

Those who were left were gathered into the market place. "You have but one choice," the Pasha told them, "to convert to Islam or die."

Lest they needed any further persuasion the Pasha instructed an apostate priest to preach to the remaining Christians. "Abandon the Christian faith," said the former priest. "Spurn the Church, and become Muslims. In return, you will be honored by the Pasha and receive many benefits."

There among the faithful, was one, a certain tailor named Pezzulla, who was a brave man and true to his faith. Pezzulla urged on his compatriots. "Now it is time for us to fight to save our souls for the Lord," he said.

"And since he died on the cross for us, it is fitting that we should die for him." To which the other captives with him gave a loud cheer.

"We, too," they said, "are willing to die a thousand times for Christ."

The angry Pasha pronounced his sentence: death.

On a day like today in the middle of August, two weeks into the siege, the chronicler tells that they were led to the Hill of Minerva, which we now know as the Hill of Martyrs.

"Here it is," said the priest, showing me a little map on the back of a card. "You can visit it afterwards," he said, before going on in a quieter voice:

"The first to be beheaded was Pezzulla. After the blade decapitated him, here the chronicler relates that his body remained stubbornly and astonishingly upright on its feet. Not until all had been decapitated could the executioners force Pezzulla's corpse to lie prone.

His executioner was a man called Berserbei. Berserbei was so impressed by this he converted on the spot. "This crime is too terrible," he said. "I will not sacrifice any more Christians on my sword."

His fellow Muslims and former comrades grew angry. "Why do you mock us?" they said.

"Have you not seen this miracle with your own eyes?" said Berserbei.

But the Muslims did not see it; they set upon Berserbei and turned his own weapon on him."

"I beg your pardon," I said.

"They turned his own weapon on him," repeated the priest. "They impaled him on his own sword."

I looked into the priest's eyes, but I could not see any irony there.

"What happened then?" I asked.

"After the siege", the Priest went on again calmer, "the Pasha attacked other towns in the territory. He took Brindisi, Lecce and Taranto. But the Christians fought back and returned to lay siege to our town.

After a second assault, if memory serves me, in September of the following year, they breached the walls and set upon the Turks. Here the chronicler relates that none of the Turkish garrison survived."

"They got their just desserts," I said.

The priest nodded.

"There is something else, however, something that is not related in the chronicle, but in another perhaps later account.

"In the aftermath of victory, the new archbishop was determined that the martyrs should be not be forgotten. He ordered his men to open up the mass grave and collect the bones of the victims of the Pasha's aggression.

When they had done this, the archbishop asked:

"How many bones can you count?"

The men went away and counted the bones. "There are too many bones," they said. "We have lost count."

The archbishop insisted:

"How many did you count?"

"More than two hundred."

"Go away and count the bones once more."

They came back to him again. "How many bones did you count?"

"*Sua Santità*," they replied, "there are more than two hundred and fifty bones."

Again, the archbishop told them to go away. Finally, they came back with the number that satisfied him.

"*Sua Santità*, we have counted more than eight hundred bones."

"That indeed is a number fit for our martyrs."

"Now," said the archbishop, "since the apostles were twelve and Christ was one, we will carve a stone in memory of the eight hundred and thirteen martyrs."

When the priest finished his story, he asked me if I would leave a contribution for his coffers.

"Truthfully," I said, as I placed several thousand lira notes in his money box, "I am not a Turk, but would you marry me in your church?"

The priest laughed.

"Only if you convert to Catholicism," he said.

I did not know which had made me feel more uncomfortable, the reliquary with the skulls and bones of the eight hundred and thirteen martyrs or the power of the priest's conviction that Catholicism was still the only form of Christianity.

You and Her

The school used to give us a cheque, every month, to cash in the Banca Commerciale. By the end of the month I was always a bit short of cash. Although I kept something back in an envelope that slotted into the upright desk in my room (I trusted Katarina and Amelia implicitly), that month I had little more than ten thousand lira (about ten pounds) in the kitty.

Arriving at the booth, the clerk scrutinised my cheque. Then he asked for my passport and went off to make a photocopy.

"I'm sorry," he said on his return, "the cheque is not valid."

In those days, my Italian was decidedly scrappy and immediately it began to falter. I called for the clerk's capo, which in some ways was like calling for the mafia.

Then I remembered I should have been using lei and not tu. For me tu and lei might just as well have been you and her.[1]

Just as I was floundering between my capos and my poorly conjugated leis, I espied a besuited friend. It was the lawyer, Avvocato Cassa.

"Professore," he said, "how nice to see you."

I explained my predicament to Avvocato Cassa.

"*Lei è il responabile?*" he said, turning to the man who had appeared from the back office.

"*Avvocato, mi dica.*"

In a matter of minutes, the problem with my bouncing cheque had been cleared up by my lawyer friend.

The responsabile smiled and shook my hand. "*Chiedo scusa per questo malinteso,*" he said. "I'm sorry for this little misunderstanding."

Avvocato Cassa and I adjourned for a coffee in the bar across the road.

---

[1] In Italian the pronoun lei is used for the third person "she" as well as formal address to all persons.

"My friend, I can't thank you enough," I said, as we sipped our coffees.

Avvocato Cassa smiled.

"One can draw a lesson from this," he said. "In dealing with persons in authority, it is better to think of them as her and not you."

Badge of Honour

I can never really relax beforehand; I am always looking round for something to do, even if I will invariably end up winging it; when my tax card came in the post that morning, I thought I had found the perfect conversation piece.

"It's been the running joke of my life here," I said at the beginning of the lesson. "I applied for my tax card about seven years ago. Although I had the number, they never bothered to send me the card. Can you believe it? I've been waiting seven years for this. Christmas and birthday have come round earlier this year."

Giovanni, who was one of my mature students, gave a wry smile as he appeared to catch my drift.

"Well," he said, "it seems you have got your *distintivo*. You must consider it a great honour."

"I don't get it," I said. "I am just a stranger in these parts. What's a *distintivo*?"

Giovanni smiled at my little teaching gambit. "Don't you mean foreigner?"

"You are right," I said. "I do mean foreigner. I still don't get it. What is a *distintivo*?"

Giovanni's wife, Cristina, who had just come in with a pot of tea and whose English is much better than Giovanni's, was laughing.

"He means your badge of honour," she said. "It is a fascist symbol. What's that got to do with Patrick's tax code?"

"*Cara mia*," said Giovanni, switching to Italian, "do you need to be reminded of the fact we are still living with the legacy of fascism."

"Giovanni, you are not explaining yourself," she said. "In English, please."

"What's so difficult to understand? You cannot deny it was the fascists who set up our bureaucracy."

"Patrick is a foreigner. He will not grasp your history lesson unless you tell him the story. However, you can only tell it on one condition."

"What's that?"

"You promise not to bring Kant into it."

By way of explanation Giovanni, who, as well as a historian, is also a professor of philosophy, began his story in his slow but nonetheless precise English. "It's not really a story about fascism," he said, "but rather how we southerners reacted to fascism and fascism became part of the continuing story of our psyche."

Cristina laughed. "Stop being complicated. Tell us the story."

"The story," Giovanni began, "concerns a conductor at the time of the building of FT railway line before the war when the fascists were in their pomp. This was quite a good job for a man of the conductor's background as the son of a simple countryman, or *contadino*.

One day, the conductor was walking through the train, checking people's tickets when he came to a man sitting in a first-class seat.

The conductor looked at the man's ticket. "I'm sorry," he said. "This ticket is not valid. You will have to go into the second-class carriage."

"Do you know who I am?"

The conductor looked at the man who was wearing a good suit. Sitting opposite him was a blonde lady wearing an expensive perfume. In those days, few women could have afforded such a perfume let alone the blonde dye.

The conductor, who was a stickler for the rules, stood his ground. "Signor," he said, "you may be the pope's cardinal for all I know, but we cannot have people with invalid tickets sitting in first class seats."

Incensed, the man stood up and slapped the conductor. "I have never experienced such insolence," he said. "I will report you to the station master."

The woman looked away as the red-faced conductor left the carriage, humiliated and seething inside.

The conductor went home where his mother was preparing the evening meal.

He went to get the bottle of table wine and poured himself a glass. He sat down without speaking. His mother placed the beans and chicory and bread on the table.

"Why don't you eat? *Non hai fame?*"

"I am not hungry."

"Well, are you going to sit there like a deaf mute all evening? What's eating you?"

When she learned what had happened, his mother threw up her arms in despair.

"Why did you do it?" she said. "Now you will never get anywhere."

But the conductor, son of a *contadino* was what they call a *testardo*: stubborn as a mule.

"I have my pride," he said. "I do not see why I have to suck up to the party."

"Will you never learn?" his mother said. "How can you expect to get on if you always work against them? What about your sweetheart? How do you think she will feel when you ruin all your chances?"

The conductor held his tongue, but his mother, as mothers often are here, took more than a simple interest in his career; she was over-protective, a fact that he resented deeply. Although he deeply resented his mother for meddling, he also had respect for her point of view. After his father's death, she had come into her own.

The conductor went to work as usual over the coming weeks. His mother, perhaps out of sensitivity, did not raise the matter again until, one evening, when she had cooked his favourite dish. A very simple dish, gnocchi dumplings made of flour and egg in a vegetable broth.

She had found out that there was to be a meeting in the village to which the party bosses were invited.

"*Figlio mio*," she said, "this is your chance. These people can make a difference to your future."

Her son shrugged. "What can they do for me that they haven't already done?"

"You must not be negative," his mother said. "Look, what I've got here."

"Where did you get this?"

"Never you mind."

The conductor, who always had a tendency to jump to conclusions, said:

"You went to see the priest. What does the priest know?"

"It is nothing to do with the priest."

The conductor snapped.

"Then it's that miserable black shirt who works in the mayor's office."

His mother dug in her heels.

"*Figlio mio*, you know how things work here," she said. "The secretary is a good man. He is prepared to do you a favour if we help his son find work in the railway."

They argued back and forth, but if her son was a *testardo*, she could also be stubborn. "Salvatore, you must go to the meeting and present the *distintivo*."

Against, therefore, his better judgment, and still bristling inside, the conductor went to the meeting to present his so-called *distintivo*, or badge of honour. It so happened that at the meeting that evening was the very man he had insulted on the train by refusing him his first-class seat.

He looked at the badge of honour. "What's this?" he said.

"It is my *distintivo*, sir."

"How old are you now?"

The conductor held his head in shame.

"You ask us to believe you marched with Il Duce," said the party boss.

The hall was crowded and everyone was laughing. The party boss turned back to the man who everyone was laughing at. "How dare you come here and insult the memory of those who marched on Rome. Do you think Il Duce gives the badge to school children?"

Humiliated, the conductor left the party meeting.

When he got home; the conductor lashed out at his mother. "It was your idea," he said. "If I had not shown my hand, I wouldn't be in this pickle."

"Well," she said, "why didn't you talk to them at the end of the meeting? You know as well as I do, everyone wants to get into the good books of the party bosses. One has to take one's chance."

"That's right, old woman. I didn't take my chance. What are you going to do about it? Buy me another *distintivo?*"

His mother, however, had a plan to rectify the situation. "You must go and see your boss," she said. "Explain the situation. Get him to rubber stamp the *distintivo*. Then they can't say you didn't march with Il Duce."

The conductor, however, was not convinced. "My boss will not do something like that. He does everything by the book."

"Just like my son!"

"Anyway," said the conductor, "how do you think he got where he is? - By being *gentile* with people?"

"Well," said his mother, "if you continue to behave like such a sour puss, no one will want to be *gentile* with you."

"Sarcasm was in both their voices. Being *gentile* was such a loaded concept," explained Giovanni. "In English it might translate as nice and kind, but at that time and in that place it resonated with false sincerity.

With great reluctance, dragging his feet, the conductor went to see his boss, the station master. As one might expect, the station master kept him waiting while he talked to his secretaries and dictated letters to his superiors in Rome. When he entered the station master's office, the conductor was already boiling over.

The station master made a big pretence of welcoming him.

"They tell me you are doing a good job," he said. "We hear you are always on time and extremely diligent about checking people's tickets."

The station master made a show of going through his records.

"I have studied your case, however. My conscience dictates that I cannot sign the distintivo."

The conductor left the stationmaster's office. Once again, he had been humiliated. "What do I need the party for?" he told himself. "I will go home with my tail between my legs. But I can look myself in the mirror, even if I do not have the badge of honour."

The conductor's mother died a few years after this. The conductor himself got married and started a family. Over the next decade and through the long, hard years of the war, however, he received no promotion to a desk job, let alone a better line.

"The story does not end here, though," said Giovanni. "After the war, my father's position within the railway hierarchy was no better.

"An opportunity presented itself when the old station master came to see him. Togliatti and the communists were calling for "purification" of those who had been involved with the fascists.

"Salvatore," he said, "you are a good man. But you must help me just as I helped you once before."

"I'm sorry," my father said. "We both know the truth."

"What are you saying? I need your help. The Communists will lynch me."

His old boss went down on his hands and knees to get him to sign the letter, but Giovanni's father's conscience would not be pricked. He refused to sign the letter absolving the old station master of his association with the former regime.

"I have studied your case," he said. "My conscience dictates that I cannot sign."

Giovanni was silent for a moment. "My father, as I have said, was a *testardo*, stubborn as a mule…"

"Now perhaps you understand what I mean by badge of honour."

The Neighbour's Clogs

Sabi had been away on business in the north. When she got to Raff's place, he was out, so she phoned him on his mobile.

"Where are you, *amore*?"

"At the Poly. - Where are you?"

"Sitting on your bed."

"With or without your undies?"

"*Porco*, when are you coming home?"

Sabi hung up. As she did, she noticed a pair of *zoccoli*, or clogs, typically worn by Italians around the house, poking out from under the bed.

The *zoccoli* were old and worn. Her own *zoccoli* were pristine and new. Raff himself did not own a pair of *zoccoli*.

Sabi went out onto the landing and rang the neighbour's doorbell.

"Do these belong to you?" she said.

"I've been looking for my *zoccoli* everywhere," said the neighbour, hardly batting an eyelid.

If by now, of course, she had grown used to Raff's ways, when he came home from work and tried to put his arms around her waist, Sabi pushed him away.

They used to fight like cats and dogs. In spite of his peccadilloes, however, Sabi was still in love with Raff.

"I can't believe you did it with that *zoccola*[2]! She is over fifty!"

"*Dai*, Sabi," he said, "She was lonely."

Sabi shook her head and closed the bathroom door. A moment later, she came back out.

Ignoring Raff, who was lying on the bed looking miserable, Sabi went onto the landing and, for the second time that day, rang the neighbour's doorbell.

"I believe you also forgot this," she said, handing the older woman her toothbrush.

---

[2] *Zoccola* is the Italian for hussy or whore.

The Motorino

Like most young professionals, Roberta owned a motorino. If there was nothing special or flash about it, it was the sort of little motorbike that could get you from A to B.

Though she did not have much affection for it, she was attached to it for practical reasons and always made a point of leaving it in Daniele's box in the garage. But as the saying goes, it always rains *tempo da ladro*[3].

Daniele, who was a lawyer, was probably more annoyed than Roberta.

"*Ladri*," he muttered, when they found the chain had been cut and the motorino stolen from Daniele's box in the garage.

---

[3] Literally time of the thief, or time for thieving.

"Well," she said. "Can't we claim on the insurance?"

But when they searched among the papers, it turned out that the policy had run out.

"*Come siamo cretini*," Roberta said. "I cannot believe we forgot to pay."

Daniele shrugged.

"Don't look at me like that. There is always the bus."

Roberta winced: she knew it was her fault. She could not get annoyed if Daniele was being obtuse.

The bus made its slow, tortuous way as it did everyday down the avenue. All about it darted scooters; cars pushed and shoved - squeezing out space till there was none left for the pedestrians squeezing between them. As it came up to the big intersection, drivers tooted their horns up and down the traffic. They pushed and pressed up against bumpers and tried to switch lanes where it was impossible to switch lanes.

The bus sat in the middle of it all – its engine ticking over.

Roberta was standing at the front of the bus behind the driver's seat.

On one side sat a man in shirts sleeves and shades. A council worker, thought Roberta, moonlighting in his friend's insurance company. Next to him were a teenage girl and boy. The girl, who was sitting on the boy's lap, was chewing gum. Did they ever go to school? She wondered.

Opposite them was a man who reminded Roberta of one of the lobsters in the fish tank in the restaurant where Daniele and she used to go at the weekends when Daniele wanted to splash out, put on his blue blazer and pretend they were living the life of Roman yuppies. The lobster's hair was bleached from the sun; evidently, he had just stepped off the beach. He was wearing flip flops, and there was sand between the toes of his cracked feet.

Roberta had always suffered from the heat. Even though she was thin, she could never get cool. Roberta was wearing a thin dress, but in spite of her thin dress, the heat assailed her. To make matters worse, the old woman standing beside her and holding onto the side with her shopping at her feet had sweaty pits.

Roberta closed her eyes on the heat and the woman's sweaty pits.

Mercifully, the bus moved off.

A breeze blew in through the open window. Roberta could see the gap in the traffic and so could the bus driver. He pressed down on the accelerator and the bus rattled along the avenue.

Ahead of them the lights were green.

At the last minute they turned red.

The bus driver slammed on the breaks. Roberta gripped the rail with her clammy hands.

The bus gave a screech. The woman with sweaty pits fell against the bleached lobster.

She let out a cry.

"Do you want to kill me?"

"-!" The old woman continued to curse the driver while she rearranged the shopping at her feet.

The bus sat at the lights at the busy crossroads. As they waited in the heat, a motorbike came around the side of the bus and pulled up in front of them. A girl in a pair of denim shorts sat behind a clad and booted biker.

Shortly they were joined by two lads on a motorino.

Topini, thought Roberta, little mice. Thieves!

One of the *topini* must have said something because the girl on the back seemed to cling even more to the biker.

The lights changed.

The motorbike roared into life; the motorino gave a rasp and the little mice took off with a squeak.

Meanwhile the bus had set off. A gust of warm air blew in through the open window.

The bus pulled into the bus stop on the other side of the crossroads.

The doors of the bus opened.

Roberta stepped aside, as the old woman made her way towards the open door with her shopping.

The bleached lobster got off behind her. As he did, his flip flop seemed to linger in the door while the old woman struggled with the step. Roberta noticed there was a blister on the back of his foot.

She was still thinking about his blister when she heard the crack of the pistol.

Afterwards, and upon reflection, she realized she also heard shouts - those harsh, guttural sounds uttered by the *topini*. And the screech of wheels as the motorino sped off.

Suddenly everyone, including the council worker and the teenagers, were standing up by the windows.

The old woman, she saw, was sitting on the ground, surrounded by her shopping.

People were looking down from their balconies.

Roberta didn't wait to see what was going to happen. She left the bus with the other people.

"I just heard the news," said Daniele. "A gangster was shot on Corso Giulio Petroni"

"I was on the bus," she said.

"You saw what happened?"

"Daniele, it was horrible. *Ho visto il sangue.* I saw the blood."

Once again, she seemed to see the whole squalid scene before her: the two-timing council worker, the teenage truants, the old woman with sweaty pits and, finally, the bleached lobster with his cracked, sandy feet and the blister on his ankle.

"Roberta," said Daniele. "You mustn't stress yourself."

"I'm not stressing myself. I just want you to appreciate what happened."

"Of course," he said.

"What do you mean, of course!"

Roberta flew off the handle. "What kind of a boyfriend are you, anyway? You never listen. When I tell you something, you don't take me seriously."

"I am taking you seriously!"

"*Mammia mia*," said Roberta. "People die at your feet and your boyfriend thinks it's all a joke."

Roberta hung up.

Daniele rang back immediately, but she did not answer.

A few minutes later, he rang again.

"Where are you?" he said.

"I'm on my way home."

"Shall I come and get you?"

"Daniele, *sto due minuti da casa*," she said. "I'm nearly home."

She felt calmer now. Daniele sensed it.

"Well," he said, after a pause, "don't you think you should go to the police?"

"What's the point?" she said. "I didn't see anything."

Even if this was technically true, Roberta had not forgotten the number plate of her old motorino.

A Tale of Envy

I was in the middle of a translation; and, it was as a particularly tricky one, my brain was starting to fog with quibbles, so I stepped out onto the balcony and stretched. From my balcony, I should point out, if one looked left, one could make out the blue of the sea. It was a delightful view, but I knew that I had to press on with the cursed quibbles when something caught my eye.

There, down in the street, was an old man, with a stooped gait and still wearing his winter coat.

To the railings, on the other side of the road, was attached an old bicycle. As the old man passed the bicycle, he stopped and bent down by the front wheel and proceeded to let down the tyre.

I could not believe my eyes. Before going on his way, he made a particular gesture: placing his left hand in the crease of his elbow and raising his right as if to say…. I will leave to you to imagine what he said to the presumed owner of the said bicycle.

A few hours later, I was still puzzling over this incident when one of my "privates" arrived.

"Can you believe it?" I said, as he walked in through the door, and I began to describe what I had witnessed but a few hours before.

My student, Dario, who had been straining, for the last six months, to conquer an exam way beyond his elementary capability, looked at me and grimaced. "*Noi siamo un popolo maligno*," he said.

"What do you mean by that?" I asked.

He shrugged as he struggled for the words. "Do you say invidious?"

"You mean envious," I returned.

"That's right," he said. "*Il nostro invidio è molto profondo.* Our envy runs deep."

Cofi and the Lion

Leaning against the wall of the old university building, Daniel took a joint from the pocket of his wide pants.

Cofi went wide-eyed:

"You smoking that here?"

Even though it was broad daylight and people were milling about, Daniel had no compulsion about lighting the joint. Cofi kept looking up and down the street to see if anyone was coming. Daniel did not seem to be bothered. – "What's the matter? You think the lion's going to get you?"

Daniel chuckled and passed Cofi the joint:

"Here, you better have some of this to calm you down."

Hardly had he spoken when a police car rolled up to the lights.

Cofi hid the joint behind his back.

"You want to waste it," said Daniel.

Cofi waited until the lights changed. Then he handed the joint back to Daniel.

"It's got nothing to do with lions," he said, "just common sense."

A few hours later Cofi was wheeling his little trolley home in the dusk. If he had not managed to sell anything very much, he did not greatly mind.

He stood at the level crossing and waited for the *metropolitana* to pass.

The gates lifted.

Cofi wheeled his trolley over the track as cars passed around him.

He wheeled his trolley down the end of the road and turned into the square by the church.

Cofi rang Julia's bell.

Cofi smiled to himself, as her voice came over the intercom. "*Ciao, bella,*" he said, as he pushed the door and rolled the trolley over the stone step and into the dark recess of the flats.

Julia came out onto the landing to meet him.

She helped him with his trolley over the threshold and they stepped into the kitchen.

"What's cooking, my lady?"

The tomato sauce bubbled on the stove.

"Hmm, smells good."

A bag of peanuts was on the kitchen table, and Cofi started to help himself. He got a handful and poured them into his mouth. Munching away at the peanuts, he grinned at Julia.

"Just look at you," she said. "Always hungry."

"Hungry," he said. "*Ho un fame lupo*. How do you say in English? I'm as hungry as a wolf."

Laughing, Julia wrapped her arms around him and squeezed his behind.

Cofi squeezed her back. "*Bella*," he said.

"*Bello*," she replied.

Cofi felt her hand running down the front of his thin trousers, as his own hand gravitated back over to the bag of peanuts.

"Hey," Julia said, grabbing the hand. "It's either me, or the peanuts."

"Just a minute," he said. "I better turn the sauce off."

And with the other hand, he swiped another peanut as Julia walked him backwards into the bedroom and threw him on the bed.

"That will teach you to steal my nuts," she said.

Something had unsettled him in the night. When Cofi awoke and saw Daniel's lion strolling across his field of vision, as if through the shaft of light that broke through the shutters, it looked like the idlest, most indolent lion in the whole of West Africa. Cofi regarded it warily from Julia's bed. The lion cannot get me, he told himself, like a mantra.

He was still telling himself it, as he stood under the arches at the back of the station watching the downpour and Daniel came running up with a black bin bag on his back. He ducked under the arches and stopped. He walked over, nodding to the others as he went. He put the bin bag down next to Cofi's display of lighters and ray bans. He threw back his snood and grinned:

"*Cazzo!* What's happening, Cofi?"

"Can't sell a damn thing, *cazzo*."

Daniel laughed.

"You want to buy some CDs."

"What about I can't stand the rain?"

The sun came out. Some college girls stopped by, wanting to see Daniel's khanga beach wraps. Daniel cut to the chase and sold one to each. Out of pity the girls bought one of Cofi's lighters, not the one shaped like a lipstick but the one shaped like a mobile phone.

Daniel joked. "She'll be calling you up soon."

"Well," said Cofi, "I won't have any money to call her back."

"Listen," said Daniel, "you know if you want to make some real money, I can always help you."

"More than I'm getting?"

Daniel grinned:

"You want to live like a lion. You must think like a lion."

Daniel teased, but Cofi knew what he meant. "I can get some more of these lighters," he said, "and buy Julia one of your khanga wraps."

Daniel laughed:

"You can buy her a fridge if you want."

"With a freezer?"

"Cofi," said Daniel. "I'm not messing you around. You will see. It will be as easy as pie."

Cofi gave him a look. "As easy as that?"

Daniel slapped him on the back. "Tonight," he said, "I'll take you to meet Racine."

Racine's car was an old Rover, which had had the stuffing knocked out of it. The upholstery was all ripped and torn. The passenger door did not open and Cofi's seat kept sliding back and forth, as they drove to a soundtrack of Racine's improvisation, namely Yassou N'Dour and old reggae numbers from the seventies.

With the ravines at the side of them, they passed through Massafra onto a vast plain that stretched down to the coast.

When they reached Taranto, they crossed the railway and drove along the seafront until they came to the Mare Grande. Racine pulled up at the entrance to the port. "You got the documents," he said.

Cofi nodded.

"I know where I have to go."

Cofi wandered through the port, passing row upon row of containers. He found an office where he handed over the bill of lading. The clerk stamped it and asked for the money. Then he looked at the quarantine papers. "Not here," he said. "You have to go to another office to pick up your goods".

"Where is the office?"

The clerk shrugged. "In the *magazzino*."

"Where is the *magazzino*?"

The clerk pointed.

Cofi wandered outside, but soon gave up the search.

He walked back to the car.

Racine sat singing to himself and with his hands rapping the steering wheel.

Racine looked up and grinned at Cofi.

"I can't find the office," Cofi said. "This place is like a maze."

"Partner," said Racine. "It's no problem. We will go together."

Racine picked up a tape from the back seat and put it in the cassette player.

"What are you bringing that for?"

"You don't like the song."

"No, the song is okay. Do you have to bring it?"

They walked back through the port. Racine swung the cassette player in his hand. Every once in a while he would sing the words.

Cofi was beginning to think Racine was crazy. He tried to tell him to turn off the cassette player, but Racine wouldn't, so Cofi decided to do it for him. "It's better this way," he said, taking the recorder from him. "You can have it back in a minute."

The clerk glanced at the quarantine certificate.

"*Un gatto*," he said. "A cat... Ah, *si, fammi vedere*. Ah, yes, let me see."

The clerk went into the back of the office and brought out a basket.

He put it down on his desk and pointed to the place where Cofi had to sign.

Racine chuckled.

"Here, kitty, kitty!"

He picked up the basket.

"Has it eaten?" he said, turning to the clerk.

"How should I know?" said the clerk. "It isn't a restaurant here."

"*Devi mangiare, piccolo.* You have to eat, little one."

"*Poveretto*," he said, turning to the clerk. "Poor little thing. My wife will be upset if it dies of hunger."

"Well then," said the clerk. "You better buy it some catnips."

"This belongs to you," said Racine. Handing Cofi the basket, he took back his tape recorder and pressed play.

They walked out of the office and between the rows of containers where a derrick was lifting a container onto a ship in one of the berths.

Racine swung his arms in time to the music. "I love this track," he said. "It always makes me want to dance!"

Cofi heard a whistle. He looked up and saw a *carabiniere* standing between the derrick and the containers.

Racine must have seen him, too, because he started to run. The *carabiniere* did a flying tackle. The cassette recorder flew across the ground and smashed against one of the containers, ejecting the cassette.

The music stopped.

Suddenly, Cofi was surrounded.

A *carabiniere* came and took the basket off him.

"What have we got here?" he said. "A cat?"

He opened up the basket.

The cat mewed.

The *carabiniere* lifted it out of the basket. Hanging from its collar was a pendant studded with rocks.

The pendant was still glistening in his mind's eye as Cofi listened to the lawyer's brief. "*Mi dispiace*," he said. "You don't have any option under the Bossi Fini Law. They will deport you back home."

The lion might have been small, but it had got him in the end.

Lamb's Wool

If Katarina and Amelia had always felt rather sorry for Guisi, they were in two minds about inviting her to their party.

"What's wrong with Guisi?" asked Patrick.

"Nothing," said Amelia. "She's a little dull. That's all."

"She's not dull," said Katarina, "she is spectacularly boring."

"You mean she's a little dyed in the wool?"

Katarina laughed.

"It's true," she said. "She does spend a lot of time knitting."

"Well," said her sister, once Patrick's joke had been explained, "I never thought of a *zitella*[4] as lamb's wool before."

The party was already in full swing when Raff popped up with a two litre bottle of something white and fizzy and his customary honk for the two sisters.

"*Porco*!" said Katarina.

"*Maiale*!" said Amelia, which for those who don't know translates as pig in any language.

"Hello, hello," he said as if to prove the point. "Who is that standing all by her lonesome?"

"Don't touch."

"What do you mean? Don't touch."

"She's not for you, Raff."

"Yes, Raff, she is off limits," said Katarina, pulling him by the sleeve. "Come and have a drink."

But Raff was not to be thwarted. A few hours later, he was seen leaving the party with a middle-aged woman in a wool jumper.

"Did you see that?"

---

[4] Old maid.

"I don't believe it."

"Should we tell Sabi?"

"I don't think it's any of our business, do you?"

A few weeks later, Katarina and Amelia were invited for English tea. "Look what I've made," said Guisi, pulling a crazy jumper out of her knitting bag. "Do you think Raff will like it?"

Neither sister liked to say it, but you couldn't get someone like Raff into lamb's wool.

The Swimmer

By his own estimation of the waters you did not need to know much about Piero to know things were looking decidedly lumpy. His wife had left him two years before for a fisherman; his one and only daughter had moved to the north – apparently also in pursuit of a fisherman; as a consequence, Piero spent most of his time fishing in the bars of the old town.

The impresario was on the phone when Piero entered his office. He nodded and Piero sat down to wait for him to finish.

There was a tray of coffee cups and a plate with a half-eaten pastry cake. A cigar burned in the ashtray as the impresario jabbed his finger at the receiver. "*Senti, discutiamo questo dopo*. The main thing is we have the theatre booked…."

Letting the impresario's voice wash over him, Piero stared round the room, looking at all the posters on the walls. If he knew all of the acts; in fact, had even worked with most if not all of them at one time or other; tucked away in the corner, there was even one of himself in his clown's uniform. "*Il Pagliaccio*," it read, "*arriva a Carnivale. Porta tutti i bambini a vedere Piero il vero bambino.*"

(The Clown is coming to Carnival: bring the kids to see the real kid!)

Piero grimaced when he saw the poster.

The impresario put down the phone and looked up.

Piero the clown smiled back.

"*Vecchio amico, come va? Tutto a posto?*"

"*Non si puo' lamentare.* Mustn't grumble," said Piero. "*E tu?*"

"*Non c'è male*," said the impresario.

Piero asked after impresario's wife, his young children, his villa in the country. Piero did the small talk, the chitchat. "*E gli affari?* How's business?"

"*Be'*," said the impresario, "*non si può lamentare.*"

"And you, Piero?"

"Be', he said, "*non si può lamentare.* Mustn't grumble."

If they were skirting around it, the impresario finally picked up the cigar from the ashtray and raised his eyebrow in Piero's direction.

"*Quindi*," he said, "what can I do for you?"

Piero shifted uneasily in his chair. "Well," he said, "you know how it is, Tony. Since that last gig in May, I haven't had anything coming my way…. *Mi stavo chiedendo*. I was wondering if you have anything for me now."

Piero waxed about his new routine. He was going to introduce a dead parrot, he told the impresario. "It's going to be a great little sketch," he said. "The joke is I am going to try and bring it back to life."

"What, the sketch?"

"Of course," said Piero, keeping his cool, "I'm going to do that. However, I was talking about the parrot."

The impresario drew on his cigar. The cigar had gone out.

He reached for a lighter and held the flame over the cigar. It took several puffs before he got it to light.

Piero broached the subject of a TV slot. "If I can raise my profile," he said. "You could get me more gigs."

He looked at the impresario.

"Piero," he said, dragging once again on his cigar, "you know how it is…"

Yes, thought Piero, of course I know how it is.

The impresario began to reel off names that were both familiar and unfamiliar to Piero: Mago Forrest, the bungling magician, La Buffala, the loudmouthed Neapolitan, Toto e Tata, this week's flavour of the month… He talked about dates, fixtures. He might as well have been talking about fittings and inside leg measurements.

The phone rang.

"Excuse me, Piero…"

The impresario took the call. His voice boomed down the phone. *"Cazzo! Cos'è successo? – Beppe!"*

Piero felt sick to his stomach…

He did not bother to wait this time for the end of the phone call.

He stood up, waving to the impresario.

The impresario looked up but did not wave back as he left the office…

Piero walked down towards the seafront. In Bar Piccolo he bought a beer and stood in silent communion with

Fredo at the bar until the old lawyer Menzini wandered in, cigarette in hand.

The lawyer ordered an apertivo and stood coughing his lungs out. Once he got his voice back, he began, as was his custom, to cast ironic aspersions on the competence of the tribunal clerks.

"*Sono pagliacci!*" he said. "They're a bunch of clowns, if you will pardon the expression, Piero. But when will they ever find those documents? It doesn't make any difference. Five, ten days. The answer's always the same. Come back in five, ten days."

Piero shrugged.

"Clowns shouldn't be working in the Tribune, *avvocato*."

The old lawyer started chuckling. As he did, he began to cough again.

They waited for him to overcome his faulty lungs. If smoking was now banned, no one, least of all Fredo was willing to stop the old lawyer committing his oldest vice.

"Well," the lawyer said finally, "it's more like a circus than a law court. *Ma cosa dobbiamo fare?* But what can we do?"

"Indeed, *avvocato*, what can we do?"

Someone came into to buy a scratch card. Fredo went round the back of the shop.

Piero nodded to Fredo; he saluted the old lawyer and walked back out onto the street. He cut across the piazzetta and crossed over the main road. He walked up towards the old town. Here, in the *N'derr la lanz*, on the side of the road, he bought some mussels from one of the fishermen.

He watched him open the mussels onto a plastic plate. The fishermen worked fast, slipping the knife between the edges of the shell. "*Vedi come sono buone,*" he said.

Piero licked his lips. "*Sono buonissime!*"

He ate the mussels raw in their liquid and washed them down again with another beer.

When he had finished his feast, he took the rest of his beer and went and sat on the jetty. He looked over at the old, abandoned Margherita theatre and the Circolo Velo, hidden under scaffolding.

"Isn't it wonderful?" someone said behind him.

Piero looked round.

It was a young woman. She must have been around the same age as his daughter.

"Indeed," he said. "It's beautiful. *Molto bello stasera.*"

For a second he paused. "It almost matches my melancholy."

The young woman looked at him. "Why? Are you sad?"

"No," said Piero. "However, it is the nature of my profession to be attuned to sadness."

"What do you do?" she asked.

"I work in the circus," he said.

"Oh, I thought clowns were supposed to be happy."

"Young lady," he said. "In all clowns there is a little sadness. Only when he understands what makes him sad can a clown make people laugh."

The young woman smiled. Then she turned away to look at the view.

They sat in silence. Piero stared out to sea.

To his surprise, when he looked round again, the young woman had removed her clothes. She was sitting in her underwear.

"Signorina, excuse me," he said, turning away, abashed.

"Why should you be sorry?" was her reply. "Anyway, it's such a lovely evening I think I will go for a swim."

The young woman slipped off the jetty and into the water.

Piero watched her as she swam out between the fishing smacks and the cabin cruisers.

"Why not," he said to himself. "It's such a lovely evening."

Piero began to undress.

He took off his shoes and trousers. He folded them and put them on the jetty.

Finally, he stood in his boxer shorts.

"What do I need these for?" he told himself.

Piero slipped over the edge of the jetty and dropped into the water.

He swam out between the fishing smacks and cabin cruisers.

When he came to the end of the moorings, Piero kept swimming.

I wonder where she's got to, he asked himself.

But the young woman had disappeared.

Piero swam on, past the harbour wall.

When he looked up again, it was dark all around him.

The lights from the shore were but specks.

But he did not feel like turning back.

"It's now or never," he told himself. "It's time to let go."

"Here," said a voice. "Take a hold of this."

Piero looked up.

The fisherman was standing up in his boat with a pole. "Hold on to it," he said. "I'll pull you in."

"You must be freezing," said the fisherman. "I've got a blanket in the back. You'd be surprised how cold it gets at night."

The fisherman handed him the blanket.

"*Cazzo*," said Piero, as he sat down in the boat, "I can't even let go properly."

"Let go of what?" said the fisherman.

Baggage Reclaim

Once upon a time, in the days before we all had little wheely bins to take on Ryanair or Easyjet, Patrick had a black Roncon suitcase with a blue strap around its middle to secure it. When it did not come up on the carousel, he went outside to smoke a cigarette. Finishing his cigarette, he went back into the airport to search for the baggage reclaim office and put in my claim.

"No," I said, "that's not mine."

"You are Signore Kavanagh?"

"Yes," I said, "but that's not my case."

The courier looked down at his paper. "You are Signore Kavanagh?"

"Look," I said, pointing at the crumpled green shoulder bag at the courier's feet, "there is the nametag. It says Signore Cardinale."

The courier looked down at the bag. "Yes," he said helplessly from behind his horseshoe moustache and shades, "but will you take the bag?"

"Can you believe it? I have to spell it out for him: he has to go back to Signore Cardinale with the crumpled green shoulder bag and come with my black Roncon suitcase, the one with the blue strap around its middle to secure it?"

Gavin chuckled

"That's nothing," he said. "My case went missing for over six months. When it got back to me, it had rubber stamps from India and Nepal."

"Touché," said Patrick, clinking his glass. "We shall have to organize a trip to India and Nepal just to see if the bags turn up. Do you want another? Of course, you want another."

"Touché," said Gavin, who was already thinking of the lump of Nepalese Red in his pouch. "By the way, did you get your case back?"

"No," Patrick said, "but I've still got Signore Cardinale's."

"If we want things to stay as they are, things will have to change." *Il Gattopardo*, Giuseppe di Lampedusa.

***

The Irish Leopard

Without a doubt Gavin Brady was a product of that mythical time in the faculty when it was enough to flash your Irish passport and the professors would assume you were a literary descendant of James or Joyce. Indeed, Gavin had been around such a long time he had become part of the furniture. As one of the DP wags insisted, he was like one of those leopard skin rugs brought back from a safari by a colonial relative. Patrick laughed when he heard this. "Gavin," he said, "may have acquired a leopard skin; nevertheless, he is still very Irish in his soul."

"So what you're saying is I won't get the contract unless we do what that so-called lawyer says?"

"Gavin, think about it."

"Well, what difference does it make? We won't clash. We'll all get our *continuità didattica*, whatever that means."

"Gavin, we've got to look after our own interests."

"I'm not saying anything. You know what I think about it, however. I am sick of their sordid little power games."

"You'll see, Gavin. Nothing will change. We'll get what we want as long as we stick together."

"Is that supposed to fill me with confidence?"

"Gavin, I'll see you tomorrow. Now go home and get a good night's sleep."

Gavin did not heed Patrick's advice; instead, he stopped off at the Maltese run by his friend, Big Paul. When he saw Gavin, Big Paul beamed and brought his hand over the bar. Gavin gripped it and beamed back.

Big Paul did not need to ask what he would like to drink. Gavin watched Big Paul pour the warm beer into a proper pint glass; his mouth watered.

He took off his jacket, and took out his mobile and keys. He put the keys and the mobile on the top of the bar. He slipped the jacket over the seat of the barstool and sat down to chat.

The Maltese became busy as it always did after eleven. Students came from all over the town to hang out listen to Big Paul's jukebox and hold forth in front of the bust of Karl Marx.

Gavin was in a better mood, and this was not just for the beer. One of the bar staff was leaving to join her boyfriend in the north, and Big Paul was looking for someone to replace her. Big Paul joked:

"What about it, Gavin? I'll pay you in beers."

Gavin thought about it for a second and laughed.

"You better pay me in cash," he said. "I'll drink you out of beers."

Big Paul handed Gavin the second beer. Gavin said:

"*Imbroglione*! What's your game, Big Paul? There's too much head."

Big Paul took the beer, and skimmed off the head. Then he poured some more head into the glass and waited.

Gavin settled down for his second pint. For a while he enjoyed the thoughts conjured by his beer. He was just thinking how nice it would be to work behind Big

Paul's bar when some old friends showed up. "*Gavin, da quanto tempo!*"

"*Vecchio amico, che fai di bello?*"

They invited him to come and sit down at one of the tables out the back.

"*Dai, vieni a prendere qualcosa con noi.*"

Gavin thanked them. He was happy to sit at the bar.

The football highlights came on the TV. Gavin watched a succession of goals. Big Paul came over and made comments about the merits and demerits of this or that team.

The bar was beginning to empty out. Gavin was just finishing his beer again and thinking about another when he looked down at the bar top. - There was his mobile, but his keys were nowhere to be seen.

Gavin tried to catch Big Paul's attention, but Big Paul was busy with a customer. Gavin's heart sunk. What was he going to do? How was going to pay the rent? How was he going to pay the bills? How would he afford Tibet? How would he fly to Mars?

All these thoughts, both bitter and ironic, seemed to flit through his mind when he saw Little Paul coming towards the bar with a tray load of empties.

"What did you do with my keys?" He said.

Little Paul looked confused.

"*Non ho capito*, Gavin," he said. "*Cosa intendi?* I don't understand Gavin. What do you mean?"

Gavin pulled his sleeve and leaned towards him.

"Where are my keys?" He said. "*Dove hai meso le chiavi?*"

Little Paul looked at him with a puzzled face.

"You've got them, haven't you?" Gavin said. "I saw you take my keys."

He looked round and called to Big Paul.

Big Paul came over, and Gavin explained:

"Little Paul took my keys."

Little Paul protested his innocence:

"What would I want with Gavin's keys?"

Big Paul and Little Paul started talking rapidly and animatedly in a mixture of Italian and dialect.

"*Ma che cazz'!*"

"*Fai il bravo…*"

"*Tu, fai il bravo…*"

Gavin, however, seemed to have lost interest in the argument. He swayed as he got up from the stool.

"Gavin, where are you going?" said Big Paul.

"*A cas*", he said, mimicking their accents. "Home sweet home. Where the curry is."

"How can you get in if you haven't got your keys?"

"Excuse me, *ragazzi*. I don't give a brass monkey's arse about your keys. I want my curry."

Gavin turned and pushed past Little Paul. He walked out the door and onto the street, pushing past the students standing round the entrance to the Maltese.

They swore at him. "*Che cazz!*"

Gavin did not give a monkey's; he walked up the street and turned the corner. He walked a few more yards and found a doorway.

He watched his pee as it formed a puddle. - The puddle drained away.

Gavin chuckled to himself when he realized it was the entrance to the faculty building.

"Serves the monkeys right!"

He zipped up his flies.

As he did, he put his hand in his pockets and felt his keys. Oh, no, he thought. You bloody ejit, Gavin.

As he kept walking, his head seemed to clear in the cold, night air. And yet he did not enjoy the sensation of sobriety. Tears welled up in his eyes; full of remorse at what he'd done, he wanted to go back and apologise to his friends, Little Paul and Big Paul. They were such good mates, and always so *gentile* and kind. They kept his beer on tap and they let him sit and drink at the bar and dream of a better life…

He looked up the street; his house was five minutes from the corner.

No, he thought, as the tears streamed down his face, this is not the key to life.

Two days later, Patrick was in the Maltese with some friends from the faculty when Big Paul came up to him. "Patrick, *come va?*"

"… A gin and tonic, of course. - And for your friends?"

He came back a few minutes later with Patrick's gin and tonic and the two gin and tonics for the two young female researchers.

"Patrick, I'm a bit worried about Gavin," he said. "Have you seen him? Only he left his mobile here the other evening."

"Oh, that's so typical of him," said Patrick. "You better give it to me and I'll give it to him tomorrow when he comes into the faculty."

Big Paul did not think anything more of it when, later that evening, Gavin appeared at the bar and ordered his usual pint. After all, a leopard, whether he is Irish or Italian, does not change its spots.

"Did you ever find your keys?" he said.

Gavin nodded.

"Mind you," he said, "I can't figure what happened to my mobile. Did I leave it here by any chance?"

Brutta Figura

Guy had just been taken on as *lettore*, or reader, in the faculty of literature and foreign languages when he was asked to be part of the commission for the new research post.

One of the candidates was a young woman. She entered the room on towering heels and made a big show of tucking in her business skirt as she sat down on the chair before the commission.

If, like the other male member of the commissions, Guy was mesmerized by her performance, when it came to the English part of her exam; he inwardly groaned.

The candidate withdrew. The commission began to discuss the merits of her case.

"I'm sorry to say," said Guy. "Her English was quite terrible. It would be asking a lot to give her a pass."

The members of the commission fell silent.

Guy realized something was up when the head of department spoke up. "I think we all agree," he said, "this is a worthy candidate."

"Guy," said one of the other professors, "eighteen does seem a little low. Do you not think you could see your way to putting up her mark to twenty-four?"

University exams were out of thirty and the minimum pass mark was eighteen.

Guy shrugged. It was all the same to him.

Later, he was speaking to one of his colleagues. "The Professor was always so friendly to me," he said, "now he just ignores me."

"Oh, dear," said his colleague, when Guy had explained what happened during the exam, "you realize that girl was his niece."

"I didn't know," he said. "Anyway, she still passed."

"Of course," said his colleague, "the Professor cannot afford to make a *brutta figura* with his colleagues."

Freak Beach

The office was full.

With only one booth open there was only one thing to do. He kept calling, at the top of his voice, until they sent for the manager.

"*Ingegnere, mi dica?*"

"Who is running this place?" he said. "*I comunisti?*"

The Engineer always rose early. Though that morning he had special reason to, as he prepared his packed lunch, comprising two doorsteps of bread and tomatoes, sprinkled with oregano, and slipped it, along with a bottle of Monticchio water into his duffel bag. By the time, however, he had finished his *servizi*, it was ten o'clock and his anger still had not cooled. He was not, in his heart, litigious he told the person in the photo beside his bed.

Only the rest of the world is litigious. If the person in the photo did not exactly concur, neither did she object to his argument. Bundling his duffel bag into the boot of the car, he turned the key in the ignition. "Titti," he said to the air. "It's going to be a fine day. I feel it in my bones."

The Engineer took the sea road going south out of town. He accelerated up past Bread and Tomato Beach, tooting his horn at a car straddling the road. He just managed to overtake before the road became one lane.

At San Giorgio he joined the *statale*. He swung in and out of the lanes, overtaking lorries and holidaymakers. About three quarters of the way he stopped at the Tamoil garage and asked for ten Euros of petrol. "*Ingegnere*," said the pump attendant, "shall I wash your windscreen?"

"Not today, Mimmo," he said. "I'm in a hurry."

"Where are you going?"

"Fishing."

"*Chi dorme non piglia pesci,*" said the pump attendant. "He who sleeps never catches fishes."[5]

---

[5] Or as we might say, the early bird always catches the worm.

The Engineer waved as he got back in his car and rejoined the *statale*.

There it was, as he came over the rise, just beyond the sloping olive fields: the sea!

The Engineer left the *statale* and took the c*omplanare* that ran parallel with the olive fields to San Vito. There were several tracks. Shortly, he saw the green dustbin that marked the turning. He slowed as he came up to it and turned down the dusty track, on either side of which was a crumbling drystone wall where sprouted prickly pears.

Cars were already parked along the track. In spite of this, the Engineer managed to find his spot under the shadow of the pine trees.

He picked up the silver sunshade from the back seat and placed it across the windscreen. Then he went round to the boot to get his gear.

Walking down the final stretch of the track, he came to the sandy cove where people lay among the beached fishing boats and the seaweed.

The Engineer walked for about five minutes, keeping to the path at the top of the rocky beach from where he would pause from time to time to enjoy the view.

On the downward path, he could see *punto piatto* where the rocky beach flattened out before the inlet.

The Engineer was in for a surprise. Most people could not be bothered to walk this far down the beach, but today *punto piatto* was occupied. In a depression, a few metres down from the path, was a makeshift *capanna* or shack, made of bamboo shoots and dry palms.

As he approached, the Engineer could also make out several half naked figures, spread out on the rocks around the capanna. A black Labrador poked its head above the parapet. But the half-naked figures remained supine and oblivious to his presence. "*Non hanno pudore!* No shame!" he muttered to himself as he cut down from the path to his usual spot on the edge of the "punto".

The sea, however, was in a benign mood; ripples of water lapped against the rocks.

The Engineer put on his wet suit bottoms. He unwound the little net from the float and dropped it in a puddle of water and strapped his *fucile* to the side. When he was ready, he went down to the shore holding his flippers and mask and dragging the float through the shallows above the rocks.

Then he sat down in the shallows, put on his flippers and mask and slipped over the edge of the rocks.

Once in the water the Engineer lost track of time, as he always did until the shadow of the sun played on the large boulder where he would prop his *fucile*. I must have been in the water a good five hours, he thought. *"Niente male,"* he muttered to himself, feeling the weight of the net in his hand.

The Engineer looked up towards the *capanna*. The students had multiplied, as had their dogs. Music blared out from a large ghetto blaster. A topless girl practiced juggling three balls, while two naked young men stood scratching themselves and appraising her skills.

"Scherzi, Fredo. Quella era più brava. You're joking, Fred. That one was the best."

"Chi è piu brava è sempre più brava. She's the best, no question."

The Engineer frowned at the vulgar snatch of dialogue. He took one of the octopuses out of the net and threw it from a height onto the rocks. He picked it up and repeated the process. One of the students came over in what appeared to be a loincloth.

He sat down on a rock and regarded the Engineer.

"What have you got there, Professore?"

It was one of the students. He was sitting on a rock in what appeared to be a loincloth.

"Octopus."

"*Quanti?* How many?"

The Engineer did not answer, so the student did it for him.

"Four if you include this little one…That's a good catch. Bravo!"

"And a sea bass?"

"It's not a sea bass," said the Engineer.

"Then it must be a sargo. I always get confused."

The student called over to his friends. "The Professor has caught some octopus and sea bream!"

His friends wandered over to take a look.

They watched the Engineer as he began to *arrichire* another octopus by throwing it against the rocks.

"What's he doing?" said one of the girls.

"He's tenderizing it."

"I can see that…"

"Excuse me," said the Engineer. "I need to get my things."

The girl was standing in the Engineer's eye-line. She was wearing crotchet bikini bottom, no top.

"*Chiedo scusa*," she said, stepping out of his way, as the Engineer rummaged in his duffel bag.

"What's he up to now?"

The Engineer filled a plastic bag with sea water. He shook the bag back and forth.

"*Geniale*...It's like a washing machine," the girl said, giggling. "Now we know what to do with our dirty undies."

So began the occupation of *punto piatto*.

They were not communists, but they might have been the children of communists. They called themselves freaks.

It was such a perfect word to describe these hairy topless girls, and hairy bottomless boys with their noisy guitars and dirty noisy dogs. Freaks!

If the Engineer was disgusted by such exhibitionism, however, he refused to buckle. He continued to fish through the summer, stubbornly refusing to vacate what, after all, was the best place to fish. He was damned if he was going to move away from *punto piatto* for the benefit of the freaks.

The office was still full.

With only one booth open there was only one thing to do. He kept calling, at the top of his voice, until they sent for the manager.

"*Ingegnere, mi dica?*"

"Who is running this place?" he said. "*I comunisti?*"

"Engineer," said the manager, "I can assure you that there are no communists in this office. *Come posso aiutarla?*"

"If you are not communists, you must be freaks. How long do I have to wait to get served around here?"

The Engineer went down to the water's edge. He took his float and dropped it in the puddle. He put on his wet suit bottoms. "Titti," he said to the air and the photo in his mind's eye. "It will be good day. I feel it in my bones."

"*Chiedo scusa, professore…* Do you have a needle?

The Engineer looked up. Squinting into the sunlight, he saw a young Tarzan. It was the boy in the loincloth.

"A needle?" he said. "What do you need a needle for?"

"It's my friend, Titti," said the boy. "She's trod on a sea urchin."

"Davide, *sto morendo*. I'm in agony," said the girl, hobbling up behind him. "Has he got the needle?"

The Engineer searched in his duffle bag.

"Here," he said. "You better sit down on that rock."

The girl did as she was told. "Give me your foot," he said.

The girl winced.

"It's painful."

"My wife used to say all medicine is painful otherwise it is not good medicine"

The Engineer removed the *spina*. "Here it is," he said. "I got most of it."

The girl smiled and thanked him.

"It's nothing," he said. "Remember when you get home you must bathe your foot in soap and warm water."

"Of course, *professore*."

She got up and put her foot down on the rocks.

He watched her as she went back up to the capanna.

A few moments later, she came back with a piece of foccaccia.

"*È fatta in casa*," she said. "I made it myself. Would you like to try some?"

"*È buonissima*," said the boy, Davide. "We've got some sea urchins."

"Well," said the Engineer. "We better be careful with the *spine*."

The Engineer fetched the knife from his duffle bag and proceeded to cut them open. The boy, Davide worked with his own knife. "Not like that," said the Engineer. "Like this."

The Engineer showed the boy Davide what to do. When they had finished cutting open the sea urchin, the Engineer lifted up some small rocks and fished around until he found what he was looking for. "Salt and pepper."

The boy Davide and the girl Titti laughed.

"*Ragazzi,*" said the Engineer, "if this is the kitchen, here is the dining room. We have of course the sea view."

A few days later, the Engineer was driving along the complanare when he saw the mini-bus.

It was parked behind a gate that led down one of the tracks. There was a group of young people standing by the gate, including the boy, Davide and the girl… Titti.

The Engineer pulled up at the side of the road.

"*Ragazzi,*" he said, *"cos' è successo?*" What's happened?"

"They have locked the gate."

"Well," said the Engineer. "Let me see about this."

The Engineer went round to the boot of his car and rummaged around.

"*Eccolo,*" he said. "Here it is. The communists have no right to block the access to freak beach."

Everyone clapped and shouted:

"*Bravo, professore!*"

The Engineer took the bolt cropper and snapped the padlock.

The students opened up the gate and drove off, waving and smiling.

Although he struggled to admit it to himself; when the Engineer got home, the woman in the photo had a smile for him, too.

The Maître D's Gaff

It is a well-known conceit of Italian life that both husband and wife are happy to take a lover or a mistress, but neither are willing to contemplate divorce, since neither wishes to upset the equilibrium in which the other lives.

The case of the lawyer Pelligrini, esteemed colleague of Avvocato Cassa, who had arrived with his wife and two young children in a smart restaurant on the Costa Merlata will serve to illustrate the point.

"*Buonasera, avvocato.*"

"Luigi."

Smiling, the maître d' led the lawyer Pellegrini to a charming and intimate corner of the restaurant where a young lady was sitting in a Versace dress, surrounded by honeysuckle and vines.

"*Penso di non*. I don't think so," said the lawyer Pelligrini. "We will need a bigger table this evening."

"Of course, *avvocato*," said the maître d'.

Realising his mistake, the maître d' led the lawyer over to a table in the middle of the restaurant.

"*Papa! Voglio mozzarella e pomodoro.*"

Avvocato Pelligrini smiled at his young daughter. "*Certo, piccola*," he said, as his wife lifted their son onto one of the chairs.

"We'll have the antipasti. But no *pesce crudo*," he said quickly. "The children don't like raw fish."

"Of course, *avvocato*. *Pizza Margherita?*"

"Good idea. We'll have the antipasti, followed by two small Margheritas, and a bottle of your house red."

"While you are about it," said his wife, "can you bring a cushion for my son?"

The maître d' nodded and gathered up the menus.

As he walked away, he smiled to himself ruefully. On his previous visit to the restaurant, the *avvocato* had ordered a platter of raw fish, followed by freshly caught *aragosta* and the most expensive of the Brunello wines in the cellar. On that occasion, however, he had been accompanied by the young lady in a Versace dress.

The Proof

The traffic was in a slow burn, backed up about a hundred metres from the lights to the barracks. Cars drifted in and out of lanes; mopeds cheeked between lines of their own invention, and yet the filter right was still blocked. Finally, the old man lost all patience and started tooting his horn. "*Cretini, sbrigatevi!*"

A car pulled out in front of them from the side road.

The old man put his foot down; they lurched forward and nearly went into the back of the offending Fiat. "*Cretino!*" said the old man, turning to his passenger. "Did you see that?"

Gabriele said nothing.

The lights changed; cars moved off. The traffic eased.

They drove along the sea road past the used car lot and the dairy where no one ever seemed to fetch the milk. Up past the boarded-up factory and the shacks where the whores plied their trade Gabriele turned and looked out at the sea. The sky was dark, and he thought it would probably rain.

The fish shop on the sea side was closed. Nobody was sitting on the slab of concrete set as a picnic table on the rocks.

The old man turned off the sea road; they went down a narrow lane surrounded on either side by the high walls of the villas and summer lets.

Turning into a cul de sac, the old man pulled up at the gate of the villa; he got out and went to open up.

The drive was like a junk yard. Leaning against the wall, behind an armchair that had had the stuffing knocked out of it, was a mattress with a brown stain.

A large red-faced woman came out of the basement flat. She called to the old man who called back. "Virginia! Come here and help me get the wine."

"I'm putting the washing out."

"Forget about your knickers. Come and help me with the wine."

Gabriele turned away in disgust.

"What's she doing in the flat?"

"She hasn't got anywhere to stay."

"Well, is she paying the rent?"

"She's got a contract."

"And you signed it?"

As they drove back into town, it had started to rain.

The old man found a parking space behind the barracks. Gabriele got out of the car and walked off down the street. His father called after him. "Where are you going?"

Gabriele did not bother to answer.

It began to bucket down. He got soaked.

When his sister came home, she found him shivering by the gas fire.

"Gabriele, *che fai*? – *Vuoi bruciare le gambe*?"

Gabriele did not say anything; he sat there warming himself by the fire.

When Vito received the call from Gabriele's sister, he left his cubby hole in the archives of radiography and went straight to cardiology.

Gabriele was already in the sterile unit. Vito put on a pair of green overalls and clogs, and buzzed the intercom.

Gabriele was lying with his head back. A drip was attached to his arm and leg.

Vito took the x-ray out of the yellow envelope and held it up to the light.

"*Gran figlio di puttana,*" he muttered under his breath. There were tears in his eyes, as he sat down on the chair beside the bed.

Vito had known Gabriele since *Lycée Scientifico*. Once upon a time, Gabriele had been marked out for brilliant things. He excelled at school and sports. He swam and fished better than all his companions. And yet, when his mother had died, something happened to Gabriele. He was no longer feisty, but seemed to lose heart and became depressed. Vito recalled the evening Gabriele came to see him in an excited mood. "Here is all the proof you need," he had said, handing him a clutch of papers. "*Dio non esiste.*" Vito, who was no longer a Catholic, but a convert, looked at Gabriele as if he was joking. He thought Gabriele's proof was quite mad and he told him so. Sarcasm crept into their voices. The argument became heated. Vito had said a few home truths. Since his mother's death, Gabriele had not done a single exam at university. He was turning into a lazy and resentful person. Gabriele stormed off. If, after that, their friendship had never quite been the same, Gabriele seemed to reconcile himself to Vito's choice. "At least, you chose your religion," he would say, "unlike all the rest of the sheep."

In the corridor outside the sterile unit, Vito bumped into Gabriele's sister.

They embraced.

"I've just finished work," she said. "*Dimmi che non è grave.* Did you see the x-ray?"

Vito described the dissection that had spread down the left-hand side of Gabriele's body.

"Nobody saw it before?"

Gabriele's sister stared in disbelief. "*Vogliano far mourire mio fratello.*"

"You mustn't think that," he said. "I am sure they are doing everything they can."

Gabriele's sister shook her head. "I should have listened to him," she said. "He didn't want to come back here to die."

Gabriele had woken in the middle of the night with a sharp pain in his chest. At the arrival of the ambulance he had not wanted to go to hospital.

"I had my work cut out," she said. "He doesn't care anymore."

"You mustn't lose heart," Vito said. "Gabriele is pretty stubborn when he wants to be."

Gabriele's sister was in tears. "*Lo sapevo*," she said. "*Non vuole vivere più.*"

Vito did not know what to say, so he changed the subject.

"*Tuo padre?*" he asked. "Does he know?"

"No," she said, wiping her tears, "nobody's told him yet. We are all worried about his heart."

"Sooner or later," said Vito, "someone is going to have to tell him."

Although busy, over the next few days, Vito kept up his vigil beside Gabriele's bed. There seemed to be no change; Vito was prepared for the worst when, to everyone's surprise, Gabriele woke up from the coma and asked for a cup of tea.

"Tea! He never drinks tea."

Gabriele's sister was laughing as they stood outside the sterile unit.

"What did I tell you?" said Vito. "He's pretty stubborn when he wants to be."

"Stubborn as a mule."

"What about the old man? Have you told him yet?"

Gabriele's sister nodded. "He doesn't want to come to the ward."

Vito saw the look of disgust in her face, but he pretended not to notice it. "I'll go and talk to him," he said. "He'll come round."

Gabriele's sister didn't see the point. "He's not answering the phone," she said. "He's always out at the villa with that woman."

"I promise I'll go and see him," he said. "He must come."

On the way home Vito drove to the street where Gabriele's father lived.

While he was parking his car, he saw Gabriele's father walking, arm in arm, with a large, red-faced woman. Guessing it was the woman mentioned by Gabriele's sister, he called to the old man, who turned round to greet him. "Petrosino," he said, "*da quanto tempo!*"

But Vito was not in the mood for pleasantries.

"Your son is lying in hospital," he said. "I am sure you know how serious it is."

"Of course," said Gabriele's father. "I will go immediately."

The old man turned to the large red-faced woman. "Don't stand there like a lemon. Get in the car."

"*Signore*," said Vito. "You are doing the right thing by your son."

The old man shook Vito by the hand and got in his car where the woman was waiting.

As far as Vito knew, the visit never took place. Gabriele took ill again and went back into a coma. He never woke from it.

The funeral came and went in a blur. Vito threw himself back into his work. The months passed.

In Italy it is common practice to say a *messa di commemorazione* a year after the death of a loved one. It was around this time Vito heard from Gabriele's sister. A party was going to be held out in the country. "We're going to plant a tree on my cousin's farm."

Vito thought it was an excellent idea. "Gabriele always loved the countryside," he said. "He loved your cousin's farm."

Gabriele's sister agreed. "He was happiest there," she said.

Vito had promised to come to the party, but at the last minute, he could not make it. His elder sister was not in the best of health. Money was also tight; Vito had taken on extra work at the hospital. To compound matters, his middle son was in trouble at school again. He was tired and worried when he received the call from Gabriele's sister. She was in tears. "*È l'albero,*" she said. "Gabriele's tree has died."

Vito did not know what to say. "*Non prenditi male,*" he said, not wanting her to lose heart. "We can always plant another tree."

"What is the point?" she said, crying. "He doesn't want to come back even as a tree."

Vito had just put the phone down when there was a knock on the bedroom door. It was his middle son to whom he had not spoken for several days. Now he wanted money.

"Why do you need it?"

"*Mama* said you would lend me the money."

"*Mi dispiace, figlio mio*," Vito said, shaking his head. "I don't have any money to give you. You must go out to work."

His son swore and slammed the door.

Vito was still sitting on the edge of the bed, head in hands, when he seemed to hear his friend, Gabriele, taunting him from beyond the grave. "Isn't that all the proof anyone needs? Even if you change your religion, it makes no difference. God does not exist."

The Hippocratic Oath

Margherita, who is a friend of my friend, Doctor Tom Tom, was on her way to the hospital when she received a call from one of her patients.

"Valentino," she said, "*Cosa vuoi?* What do you want?"

"Dottore, can we speak confidentially?"

"I'm on my way to work," said the doctor. "What can I do for you?"

"Dottore, I won't beat about the bush. I don't like the look of my pee."

"What's wrong with it, Valentino?"

The patient began to describe his symptoms. Margherita listened with her eyebrows raised.

"Valentino," she said eventually, "as you know, there are cures these days for things like that."

"Dottore, that is a relief."

"Now listen, Valentino. Have you told Ines?"

"Of course not."

"Valentino, what do you mean? You haven't told her. You must tell her."

"Absolutely not. Ines mustn't know. She will kill me."

"Well, have you had *rapporti* with her recently?"

"No."

"Valentino, be honest. When was the last time you had *rapporti?* "

"Okay, I admit, it was last week."

"Well," said Margherita. "That's something. At least you are doing your duty."

"I always do my duty," said the patient.

"Valentino, you know what your duty is now. You must tell Ines."

"Dottore, it is *fuori discussione*. Ines mustn't know."

"Well, in that case," said Margherita, "what do you think I should do about it?"

"Nothing," said the patient. "It is imperative you keep your Hippocratic Oath."

Margherita sighed. "Come and see me at the hospital this afternoon."

The patient hung up. A second later, the doctor was back on the phone to her patient Ines.

When she finished her call, she looked around at the bus. "Beh," she said, "what does he expect me to do in the circumstances? Keep my Hippocratic Oath?"

The bus nodded in appreciation. No one wanted an outbreak of the clap on the streets of Naples.

Bermuda Triangle

It looked like it was going to rain, but, of course, it never did. The clouds would not budge, but nor would the heat. They could not stay a moment longer in the flat, so they bought a wheel of foccaccia and a bottle of Guadianello and went to the beach in Torre a Mare.

They parked the car where the road ended in a cul de sac and up on the cliff was a Second World War pillbox sprayed with graffiti: Forza Juve, Lecce Merde, and Vafanapoli...

What the devil was that all about?

The sea was perfectly still and people were bathing in the cove, so they walked onto the next cove and climbed down the old rusty steps onto the sand.

They made a place for themselves among the seaweed and the sand flies and spread out Julia's towel.

Julia took off her top and went to the water's edge. He watched her as she stood in the shallows. After a while, she waded out and dropped down into the water.

"Aren't you going in the sea?" she said.

But Daniel had other things on his mind.

Behind them, there was a hollow in the rocks. They manoeuvred the towel and themselves into the hollow. There they lay among the flotsam and jetsam: pieces of old rope and netting, blanched wood, plastic bottles and cups. He crouched over her and helped her as she eased down her bikini bottoms. He put his hand on her freckled chest where she was almost dry; then he put his hand between her legs where she was wet.

The first time they made love was on the beach. The second time they were in the flat.

The salt had dried on her skin. He lay panting as she got up and went into the bathroom.

He lay on the bed, listening to her as she turned on the shower.

She came back into the bedroom and lay back down on the bed. When they started again; slowly, then suddenly quickening their pace, the soap and the shampoo did not make any difference. They were both dripping with sweat, when he felt it: something twisted inside him.

"Why don't you go ahead?" the voice said. "She deserves it."

When Cofi was arrested, Daniel had gone to see the priest at Santo Stefano. The priest had said he would do what he could for Cofi; then he had invited Daniel to pray.

Daniel was not a believer, but he had sat in the pew next to the priest while he did. If he knew it was just to salve his conscience, when things had precipitated with Julia, he knew that his conscience had nothing to do with it.

"What is the matter, Daniel? Don't you want to anymore?"

"I'm just tired," he said. "That's all."

Daniel did not as a rule remember his dreams, but he awoke with this one clear in his mind. The reason for this was that, even if it had chosen to misinterpret it, the dream was close to reality.

Finding himself back in the boat in the middle of the sea; the boat appeared to have capsized and Cofi was struggling beside in the water. Cofi appeared to look at Daniel for help. But just as Cofi called out, the dream had displaced him. "No," the voice had said, "you cannot go back."

Julia was busy at the school, and Daniel had his own things to do. They had arranged to meet at the flat, but she was late.

"Where have you been?"

"Are you annoyed?" she said. "If you must know, I went out for a drink with one of my students."

"Who is he?"

"Actually, it was a she."

"Do I know her?"

"Why, are you already bored of me?"

She opened the door to the flat and he followed her in. She dumped her books on the table in the kitchen. She went to the bathroom. He heard her turn on the tap.

She pulled the chain.

Daniel shook his head.

"You want a beer," she said on re-entering the kitchen. "There's one in the fridge door."

He took out the beer and poured it into two small glasses.

"What's the matter, Daniel?" she said.

Daniel shrugged.

"It's nothing."

She looked at him.

"If it's nothing," she said, "you seem to be making a mountain out of it…"

She lit a cigarette. As she did, she looked at him again. "You know," she said. "I only just worked it out."

"What?"

"Cofi's problem. He had a kid, didn't he, back home. It wasn't just his mum or sister, was it? There was a kid he had to look after, too. Am I right, Daniel?"

He grimaced.

"Well," he said, "you take the prize."

Daniel was suddenly agitated. It surprised him. A feeling of bitterness overwhelmed him.

He got up and went and stood over by the window. Down in the street a motorino beeped its horn. A man shouted at the top of his voice: "*Coglione!*"

Julia came to the window and they both looked out.

There was no one in the square but a group of teenage boys talking among themselves and eating *cornetti*.

Daniel sat down and sipped his beer.

"What is it, Daniel?"

He sighed.

"It's the Bermuda Triangle," he said.

"What do you mean?"

"Exactly what I said. The Bermuda Triangle."

"That doesn't make any sense to me."

"Well, let me spell out for you. I might just as well not be here. No one sees me. I walk down the street. They ignore me. I see everything they do. As they swing out of their coffee bars, mobile phones in hand and kiss their girlfriends goodbye, they pass me by. Someone might stop to look at one of my things. But they don't see me.

They don't hear me when I tell them how much it is. My invisibility precedes me. So that is why I tell myself. I am living in a Bermuda triangle."

Daniel fell silent.

He waited to see what Julia would say. But she said nothing; instead, she asked if he was hungry.

Daniel shrugged.

"Well, I'm hungry," she said. "Shall we go and get a piadina?"

The pizzeria was packed: old folks and their friends, birthday parties and works outings, *fidanzati* and their friends.

They watched the *pizziaolo* Enzo work rapidly to shape the dough. They watched him spade it with the flat wooden peel into the oven. They watched Luigi as he cut into the fat of the Parma ham, set it in the slicer and laid it, along with some mozzarella, out on the piadina. He took a handful of tomatoes and some rocket. Then he folded the piadina and wrapped it in the paper and handed it to them, his gold ring finger wrapped round it so that none of it toppled on the floor.

"*Buon appetito*," he said.

They took their piadinas outside and stood looking out to sea from the railings on the seafront. The air was damp and there was a pungent smell of seaweed that seemed to chime with Daniel's mood. All is rotten here, he thought. It stinks.

Finishing their piadinas, they went back to the flat, got undressed and got into bed.

Julia turned out the lights; Daniel moved towards her tentatively in the darkness.

But he found, to his distress, that she was in tears.

"Daniel," she said after a while, "I don't think this is right."

"What is not right?"

"What we are doing."

"You are worried what Cofi will think? Cofi will never know."

"Daniel, that's not the point."

"Well," he said, "what is the point?"

"Daniel," she said, "we must be kind to each other."

"At the moment," he said, "I feel as if all your kindness is a deception."

A few days later, Daniel left for the north. He had found a job working on a building site outside Milan. He worked in Milan for six months. Then he went to work for a timber merchant in Bergamot. He worked for the timber merchant for three months, but when the timber merchant stopped paying him, he left. He drifted around the northern towns, selling wares, until, one day, Bembi wrote telling him he was opening a little shop.

Daniel drifted back south, but there was not much work for him in Bembi's shop and he found himself slipping back into the old routine.

It was a Tuesday, market day in Monopoli. In the market they sold fake designer tops and fake designer shoes and pretty fake underwear for the ladies. Daniel liked to peruse the stalls, scrutinizing all the high-end fakery. Around midday he would go to the deli man, Nicola and get him to make a sandwich with Parma ham and fontina. Then, as it was autumn, he would buy some persimmon from one of the fruit stalls.

When he had had enough of selling his wares, Daniel would walk down through the boatyard and sit on the rocks to eat his sandwich. Here wild thyme grew among the rocks and the water lapped on a small sandy beach.

The days were still warm. Daniel was content and, in his contentment, everything seemed to open up for him. He no longer felt, as he had done since that day with Julia, lost in a Bermuda Triangle of his own making.

Stiletto

Often people will drop things. It is one of the hazards of living in a block of flats. Pegs break, especially the new plastic ones, which is why he preferred the old wooden pegs. A t-shirt or one of a pair of stocking socks or a pair of no-nonsense knickers can find their way onto one's balcony but this was getting ridiculous...

It had been six months since Signor Campobasso, who is a retired porter, started receiving what he described as the "trophies" on his ground floor balcony.

"Who do you reckon it is?" he said.

His neighbour, Schino, whose wife had Alzheimer's, shrugged.

"You think it could be one of the *studentesse* on the third floor."

"Not exactly their style, is it."

"Of course, it could be a practical joke."

"One of the plumber's kids."

"Those little hooligans. What about the Signora on the fifth floor?"

"That old bag? I don't think she is right in the head."

"And the daughter?"

"*E buona quella*," said Schino.

"*Troppo buona.*"

They both laughed.

There was no lift in the block of flats. Signor Campobasso climbed the four flights of stairs to the top of the building.

The door was ajar.

"Signora?" he called.

When there was no reply, he pushed the door and entered.

The Signora's daughter was sitting at the end of the corridor, with her legs astride a kitchen chair.

"*Ti dispiace*," she said. "Would you mind putting it on for me?"

Signor Campobasso had no choice. He knelt at her feet with the other stiletto on his back…

Suddenly he could not breathe.

Signor Campobasso opened his eyes. He was standing on his balcony with a clothes' peg over his nose.

Those ruddy plumber's kids, he cursed.

If you go chasing rabbits
Tell 'em a hookah smoking caterpillar
Has given you the call – Jefferson Airplane

***

Chasing Rabbits

"*C*iao, *cugi*!" Dino had paid one of his flying visits. He'd brought with him provisions: aubergines, courgettes, Zia's homemade *passata* of tomatoes, *salsiccia lucana* and a whole rabbit. "Don't put it in the freezer," he said. "It's already defrosting."

A few days later, he asked Paige:

"What did you do with the rabbit?"

"I threw it away."

"Why did you do that?"

"It was beginning to smell."

If Guglielmo was annoyed, he did not say anything; instead, he picked up the car keys from the side.

"Come on," he said, "or we'll be late."

"I'm ready," said Paige. "In fact, I've been waiting for you."

"*Andiamo,*" he said.

"*Si, andiamo.*"

The gig was in an old wine cellar. On the back wall, behind the band, was a blazon with two crossed spears that seemed, over the protest of banjo and harmonica, to challenge Guglielmo's mood. After a while, he went outside to smoke a cigarette.

When the gig was over, they hung around with Scott and the other members of the band drinking beers and making small talk until Paige decreed it was time to go home.

"Why did you have to be so unpleasant to Scott?" Paige said.

"What are you talking about? I was just teasing him."

"William, you were not teasing him. You were being mean."

"He laughed, didn't he? Anyway, I thought they were good."

"No, you didn't."

"I did."

"They were really good. *Sono bravi.*"

"Scott has a wonderful voice."

"Certo, Scott ha una bella voce."

If she could hardly fail to pick up his sarcasm, for the rest of the journey, Paige said nothing.

Guglielmo dropped Paige off at the flat and went to park the car. As usual, he could not find anywhere near the flat and ended up parking under the fly-over the other side of the level crossing.

When he got home, Paige was already fast asleep, rolled up in a fetal ball with the cat. Guglielmo turned on the TV and rolled a joint.

Two local comics were on the TV. One of the comics was reading a poem, which seemed to involve a visit to Joe Strummer's flat in Notting Hill... He loved the silliness and obscurity of the joke. Guglielmo had never been to Notting Hill, nor had ever met Joe Strummer. But he had always loved the Clash. Unexpectedly, his eyes began to water.

Everything had seemed perfect when they were in Australia and Paige had said she wanted to experience Europe. Guglielmo had been swept up in her enthusiasm. But now they were back in Italy, it had not worked out how he had imagined it from the bottom of the world. The question lingered in his mind. Was it his fault or hers?

Paige had already left for work when Guglielmo got out of bed. He made himself a coffee and ate a piece of toast. Then he got dressed and went out. He walked down to the seafront and up to the bar by the pine gardens for a second coffee with Arturo and some of his work colleagues. Afterwards, he went to see Toni in the sports shop, but Toni wasn't around, so he went back and shot pool in the bar. This had been his routine for days. What was he doing with his time?

In the early afternoon, as promised, he went round to his sister's to pick up the kids and take them for their swimming lesson. He sat in the stand, watching them swim back and forth. "How many lengths was that?" asked Paolo.

"I counted twenty," said Lucia.

"It was more than that," said Paolo. "Wasn't it, Zio?"

"I lost count," said Guglielmo.

"You see," said Paolo. "We did loads."

"Come on," he said, "let's go and get an ice cream."

After the ice cream, he took the kids home. When they had gone off to do their homework, his sister put on the coffee and Guglielmo lit a cigarette.

"Well," said his sister, "how are things going? How's Paige?"

Guglielmo shrugged.

"She's at school."

His sister cadged a cigarette; he offered her a light.

"Guglielmo," she said, as she drew on the cigarette, "when are you going to get a job? You know papa can get you work in the post office."

Guglielmo sipped his coffee, but did not say anything.

"Guglielmo, why don't you go and see papa?"

Guglielmo was suddenly annoyed. "Frankly," he said, "I don't know why I came back here if all you can say is I should become a postman like papa. What am I supposed to be doing with my degree?"

"Well," said his sister, "if you don't get a job, why don't you leave again?"

"I might just do that."

When Guglielmo got home, Scott was sitting in a chair in the middle of the room. His hair was wet and he had a towel round his shoulders. Paige had a pair of scissors in her hands.

Scott went bright red.

Although it was immediately obvious what was happening, Guglielmo couldn't help himself.

"What is going on?" he said, turning to Paige. "Is he your boyfriend now?"

Paige tried to say something but Guglielmo was furious.

"Leave me alone," he said.

Slamming the door, he went into the bedroom where he started throwing clothes into a hold-all.

The statale was empty but for a few lorries going north. From the statale Guglielmo took the turning for Castel del Monte. The way was full of vineyards and olive groves. From the castle the road climbed until he reached the radio tower, then slowly it began to wind back down.

Guglielmo kept going across the open country.

It was only, however, when he had reached what was known locally as "terra rossa", the red lands, did he begin to relax.

He looked down across the valley. There was a mist all the way to the railway line that ran parallel with the Potenza road.

Guglielmo wound down the window and breathed in the air. Then he put on the radio. It was an old song, one his mother used to listen to.

A short while later he was driving down a bumpy track when a tractor came towards him. The tractor pulled up at the side of the track, and as he went past it, his cousin Dino leaned out of the tractor and called to him:

"*Ciao, Cugi! Che fai?*"

The farmhouse was at the top of the vale. Below it were some outhouses that comprised the cow shed and a grain store. At the bottom of the slope was a big barn where the tractors were kept.

Guglielmo got out of his car. As he did, Mussolini came over to sniff him; he went round to the boot to get the tray of *pasticinni*.

His aunt and uncle were sitting in the kitchen.

"Memo," said his uncle, getting up from his chair by the fire. "*Che ci fai?*"

"Zio," said Guglielmo, "I've bought you some cakes."

His uncle smiled and patted him on the back.

He turned to his aunt. "Zia," he said, *"da quanto tempo."*

They embraced.

His aunt was overcome with emotion.

They sat down and she made them all a cup of coffee; then he went with his uncle to look at the cows.

Guglielmo stayed the night in the loft. In the morning, he went out with Dino on the tractor to inspect the olive fields. "It's a lot of work," said Dino. "I could do with some help."

"Why not?" said Guglielmo. "My mother always loved these fields."

"Well," said Dino, "you know they are still yours."

But Guglielmo would not hear it. *"Cugi,* all that was settled long ago. Anyway," he went on, "it will be a pleasure to give you a helping hand."

"You'll see," said Dino. "We'll still get a good crop this year."

Over the next few days Guglielmo began to enjoy himself. Sometimes he went running in the country lanes. Sometimes he helped his uncle milk the cows, but most of his time was spent with Dino pruning the olive trees that once belonged to his mother.

One evening, over supper, his aunt broached the subject that was on everyone's mind.

"*Tua moglie è una bella ragazza,*" she began. "Your wife is very pretty. However, the prettiest are not always the best catch."

His uncle chuckled:

"Lucky you got me then, old woman."

His aunt looked at Dino.

"Really," she said, "anyone one would have thought he was Don Giovanni."

"Is that true, Zio? You are Don Giovanni?"

"That old fool," said his uncle, "I was always Marlon Brando."

Guglielmo laughed.

"Is it true, Zia? Zio was Marlon Brando?"

"Only his dreams!"

"*Vecchia,*" said Marlon Brando, "that was not what you said to me last night."

At that moment Dino came in with the bottle of wine he had gone to fetch from the cellar.

"What do you think?" he said.

"*È frizzante.*"

"You like it?"

"*È ottimo.*"

Dino grinned.

His aunt had cooked meatballs in tomato sauce.

They sat eating in appreciative silence.

"Zia," said Guglielmo eventually, "you have surpassed yourself. That was delicious."

"Memo, you want some more?"

She got up to fetch the dish and piled some meatballs, along with tomato sauce, onto his plate.

"You know what the problem is," said Guglielmo. "My wife does not appreciate the good things."

Then he told them about the rabbit. "Can you believe she threw away a perfectly good rabbit?"

His uncle looked nonplussed.

"Paige is a vegetarian?"

"Zio, Paige isn't a vegetarian, but she might just as well be a vegetarian."

"You understand, Zia," he said, turning to his aunt. "I married a woman who does not understand real things. How can I put this?"

He stopped in his tracks, searching for the right words.

"… She is off chasing rabbits."

The Alliance

The Condominium meeting was in full swing when the plumber stood up and walked out, followed by Signor Campobasso. The administrator was not surprised; Signor Campobasso was constitutionally incapable of attending a condominium meeting without walking out, especially where money was involved. When, however, the Professoressa also stood up to leave, he screwed up the piece of paper on which he had diligently been taking notes and turned to Katarina. "Signorina, the meeting is as good as over," he said, "we do not have a majority."

"*Cosa dobbiamo fare?* What are we going to do? The sewers are beginning to stink."

"*Mi dispiace, Signorina. Ma ciammafà,* as they say here. *Cosa dobbiamo fare?* I'm sorry to say but what can we do?"

Katarina accompanied the administrator out through the smelly courtyard when they bumped into the Professoressa and the plumber.

"It really is intolerable", the Professoressa was saying.

"I quite agree," said the plumber. "It really is intolerable."

They shook their heads vociferously but in apparent agreement.

What was going on?

"I don't get it," Katarina said as she said goodbye to the administrator. "Why are they suddenly so friendly? I thought they had been mortal enemies ever since the plumber's children put cockroaches in the Professoressa's shopping."

"It's really very simple," said the administrator. "As long as he uses her son to rubber stamp the papers down at the council office, she will give him her backing for the contract to overhaul the sewers."

"And what about Grumpy?"

"I have to agree with them," said the Administrator. "His underwear is not the prettiest sight in the block."

When Katarina got back to the flats, she noticed, under Signor Campobasso's window, a red bucket with Signor Campobasso's dirty underwear sitting in water and bleach.

Lawrence Drummond

The British was an old-fashioned sort of language school. It had that very end of Empire feel. The doors were painted blue and red, and there were framed posters of a Union Jack, maps of the London underground and photos of the Beatles in the classrooms. There was a life size poster of a Guardsman staring at you as you walked in through the door. To Dee, who considered herself an old hand at the school, it seemed, as she stood in the officer's mess of the Frigate Scirocco, the British had found its own living version of the guardsman.

In contrast to the Italian naval officers, Lawrence Drummond was a strapping fellow; he was a fair haired, broad shouldered chap in his late thirties.

"What do you think?" said Fiona.

"Well," said Dee, "he certainly cuts a dash next to this little lot."

"He told me earlier he owns a castle."

"Where?"

"Somewhere in the Highlands. It's a ruin."

"Do you believe him?"

"I doubt it. But I reckon it'll be fun finding out, don't you."

"Ladies," said Lawrence, returning with their drinks, "just been chatting to the captain."

"Oh, what he did have to say for himself?"

"I found out he was in the Gulf."

"In the Gulf?"

"Yes,

"Were you in the Gulf, Lawrence?" said Dee.

"Well, as a matter of fact, I was."

"Fought with the Kurds," he said. "Such a splendid lot. Incredibly brave."

"Incredibly brave," said Dee. "Don't tell me you were incredibly brave, too?"

Lawrence threw back his head and laughed aloud.

They said goodbye to the Captain and his officers and Lawrence escorted them, like the dashing Arabian knight he claimed to be, off the ship.

"Is that yours, Lawrence?" said Fiona as she tottered towards the car park.

"Actually, it is…I drove it over from Angleterre."

"I've never been in a jag," said Fiona. "Come on, Dee. What's keeping you?"

She turned round to find Dee tugging at one of her heels. "I can't be bothered with these pumps anymore," she said.

When she saw the Jaguar, she said:

"Crickey, Lawrence, will you let me drive?"

Lawrence laughed.

"Actually," he said, "it's not really worth a bean. I've had it about sixteen years. Would you care to hop in?"

Here began a series of episodes that seemed to be inaugurated by Lawrence sweeping them off in his white jag to an amusing world of his own conjuring. They drove down the coast and found a beach bar. Lawrence decided he wanted a swim. He stripped off his clothes and waded out in his boxer shorts. They drove back into town and sat in one of the up all night bars on the seafront singing songs Lawrence said his father sang to him on cold, windy nights beside a blazing fire. Around five o'clock in the morning he took them for champagne breakfast in the Hotel Orient. Lawrence became etched on Dee's mind, like some preposterous figure of fun, swaying with his cigars and his shots of whisky or grappa in a pair of boxer shorts until the delicious moment when they met the Yorkshire choreographer in the Bohemien who professed to be on a grand tour of the "Bel Paese" in his boyfriend's yacht. "Why don't you come with us, darlings? I am sure we can all squeeze in?" If, as it seemed, they would sail down the coast to the tune of some magic nocturne, finally, they returned, like two punch-drunk sailors, to Dee's flat where Lawrence threw off his clothes, shook briefly and finally collapsed on top of her. "What's that?"

Dee felt something cold and metallic on her chest.

"Oh, that," he said. "It is my medallion." You want me to take it off.

"Where did you get it?"

"One of my chaps gave it to me."

"One of your chaps? You do make laugh."

Lawrence sighed breathlessly.

"You don't believe me, do you, Dee? I can't help it, though. I find it easy to confide in you."

"Is that what you're doing, confiding in me? – Well, when do you plan to spill all the beans?"

"Of course not. If I was to tell you everything, I wouldn't know where to begin."

"How about the truth?"

Lawrence was silent for a while.

"Dee, can I let you into a secret?"

"What?"

"I've hocked the jag. Sold it to a student, Avocado Cassa."

"You mean, Avvocato Cassa."

"That's the one, Avocado Cassa."

"Why did you do that?"

Lawrence sighed.

"It's a long story. Let's just say there are people after me."

Dee laughed. "What? The CIA? The KGB? Mossad?"

"I'm serious," he said.

"Well," she said, "let's pretend we are both serious, shall we."

She pulled him to her and they started to make love again.

Dee had been teaching out at an engineering company in the industrial estate, so she did not have cause to go into the school until much later.

Fiona was in the staff room.

"You've missed all the fun."

"What's happened?"

"The petty cash box has been stolen."

"You're joking."

"Teresa was in tears. She thought it was all her fault, when she came in the morning and found the box open in Leo's office.

"Leo and Virginia are very upset. There's going to be a meeting tomorrow."

"Oh, no… how much money was in it?"

"Virginia didn't say… She's convinced it's Lawrence."

Dee looked shocked.

"Where is Lawrence?"

"No one knows."

"You're joking," said Dee slowly.

"I am not," said Fiona. "He was supposed to come at three to do a Shenker lesson. Only he didn't."

"He didn't. He said he would."

Fiona looked at Dee and said:

"Oh, Dee, you didn't."

"You're not jealous, are you?"

"Why should I be? – Share and share alike remember."

Dee laughed.

"Well, in that case, it's alright then, isn't it?"

Dee went over to make herself a cup of tea.

She sat down and turned to Fiona:

"Well, do you reckon it was him, then?"

The incident of the petty cash box was glossed over. The money was never recovered. But no one wanted to blame Teresa. They never saw Lawrence again. If he had done a runner with the money, Dee did not feel very inclined to judge him.

A few days later, Dee was cleaning up in her flat when she found his medallion on the floor under the bed. She put it away in a drawer and forgot all about it until the day she was moving out of the flat and came across it again.

Dee burst out laughing.

"What's so funny?" said Guy, who was helping her move boxes.

She told him about Lawrence and showed him the medallion.

"Have you seen anything like it?"

"Well," he said, "it must be kismet."

"What's kismet?"

"Your destiny, or fate."

For a second she thought about Lawrence, and felt a little pang at the memory of his extravagant lies.

She was going to put it in the bin when Guy said:

"Don't you want it anymore?"

"No, you keep it."

The Convert

Bembi had had a hard winter living in a derelict house by the railway tracks when Daniel told him about the priest at the San Rocco church.

After the service the priest took him into his office and questioned Bembi about his faith. Bembi did not make any bones about it; he could not pretend to be religious. "I am planning to get religion, one day," he said. "At the moment I don't get it."

The priest laughed. "Well," he said, "let me help you try and get it. Why don't you come next Sunday?"

Bembi went back the following Sunday. The priest gave him some odd jobs to do around the Church.

The priest had a number of helpers, but Bembi had always been good at fixing things, especially cars. The Priest's car was a perennial choker. After a bit of tinkering with the carburettor, Bembi managed to get it going.

"All it needed was a bit of patience."

"I will remember that," said the priest, "and put it in my sermon."

One day, Bembi had borrowed the priest's car. When Bembi did not show up at the Church, the priest grew worried. Later, he learnt Bembi had been picked up by the police without his *permessso di soggiorno*[6] and had been taken to the camp out by the military airport.

The priest got in his brother's car and went out to speak to the Colonel who ran the camp, but it was too late. Bembi had been shunted off to a camp further south.

Six months later, the priest was coming out of church when he saw Bembi. He had the bonnet of the car up with the engine ticking over sweetly.

"All it needs is a little patience," he said.

---

[6] Leave of stay

Tutt' a Post'

La Uascezze was a bar in the old town, much in favour with the English Club and their hangers-on. Graham and Gavin and his mate, Sean, who was over for the week from Manchester, were down one end of the table drinking Effe beer when Graham leaned back in his chair. As he did, he fell backwards.

"Steady on, mate. What are you doing?"

Sean reached round to grab Graham by the shirt.

"Graham, *che combini?* What are you up to?" the amused Italian voices called from the other end of the table.

"*Ubriacone!*"

"Ubri-ac-on-e! What does that mean?!

"It means he's pissed," said Gavin.

"Graham, are you pissed?"

"Maybe a little tipsy."

"Don't look now, mate. Your girlfriend's throwing daggers."

Graham stood up and waved down to the other end of the table. "*Tutt' a post'*," he said, smiling.

"*Tutt' a post'*," said Sean, aping Graham. "What does that mean?"

"It means, everything's okay."

Sean chuckled. "*Tutt' a post'*, mate. You want another Effe."

"Better not."

"Mate, you wanna be careful. She's got you under her thumb. Wouldn't you say, Gavin?"

"That's what I keep telling him."

"Telling me what?

Sean chuckled.

"She's got you under her thumb."

"No one's got me under their thumb," said Graham.

"I'll drink to that," said Sean. "If I were you, however, I'd watch it. That girl of yours looks useful in a fight."

"What do you mean?"

"To put it bluntly, she hasn't got much of a sense of humour at the moment."

"That's what I keep telling him," said Gavin. "She doesn't do humour."

Graham shrugged.

"There's not much I can do about that."

"Yes, there is," said Gavin. "Get another girlfriend."

"I don't want another girlfriend."

"Ok," said Gavin. "Join the singles club."

"Like you. Sit around all day drinking Effe."

"Well," said Gavin, "it's better than being stuck with the Pulizia!"

"What do you mean, the police?"

"No, he means the pulizia, the cleaning."

"The cleaning?" said Sean.

"That's right," said Gavin. "That's all she does all day. Either that or she's out making a fashion statement."

"Actually," said Graham, "that isn't the only thing she does."

He winked at Sean, who laughed.

"It's bedtime stories then."

But Gavin wouldn't let go. "It's not bedtime stories," he said. "It's cleaning, cooking and parties with her cousins. Then he's tucked up in bed. No bed time stories."

"Well," said Sean, sensing the tension in the air. "As far as I can see, she's very friendly."

"That's the point," said Gavin. "She's far too friendly."

"Speaking of which, what about a friendly pint of Effe?

"A friendly pint of Effe," said Graham, giggling. "Sounds like a proposition."

"I'll get you one, then?"

"Why not?"

"And you, Gav? – Goes without saying. Three friendly pints of Effe."

He called up the table. "Ragazzi! Want a beer?"

The Italian girls smiled.

"Effe?"

They shook their heads.

Graham was deep inside his second pint of Effe when the urge came over him.

"Prepare to be amazed," he announced to his friends.

"What are you doing?"

"What does it look like," he replied. "I'm levitating."

"Levitating, mate. All I see is a guy standing on one leg."

"You are not looking from the right angle. Go and stand over there."

"You see," he said, pressing his palms together reverently. "I'm a Buddhist monk."

"More like crappist monk, mate."

Graham was even more determined when he tripped on his sandal and fell over.

"Graham, *che combini*!"

"*Ubraicone*!"

"Watch it, mate. Your girlfriend's throwing daggers again."

Graham picked himself up off the ground and waved to the other end of the table. "*Tutt' a post*," he said.

"*Tutt' a post*', said Sean.

"I need another Effe," said Graham.

He wandered off in the direction of the bar.

"*Tutt' a post*'," said Sean.

He winked at Gavin who grinned back.

"I think Graham's just got his sense of humour back."

As if to prove the point, Graham went out with them the following night and every night thereafter of Sean's stay. They got some tickets for the mid-week game and watched Edgar Davids run rings round the local football team. They hung out with Gavin's friends on the seafront smoking weed and drinking Peronis. Each night Sean insisted upon returning to a seafood restaurant known as the Credenza. On the last night he stuffed himself silly with the antipasti from the sideboard and insisted upon being wheeled home in a shopping trolley they found on the high street. By the time they had loaded him into the plane along with the ceramic plates for the misses, his bottles of limoncello and olive oil for the in-laws Gavin felt he was due for a quiet night in. But when the citofono went, he was resigned to answering it.

It was Graham's girlfriend. If Gavin was a little surprised, since there was no love lost between them, he did not show it:

"Serena, *vuoi salire?*"

"*Dov'e?* Is he with you?"

"Graham, *non c'e.*"

"*Non prendermi per il culo*, Gavin. Don't take me for an idiot."

Gavin knocked on. the bathroom door.

"Has she gone, mate?"

"You think she was going to hang around here, crying over your spilt milk."

"I didn't think so."

"Well, are you coming out?"

"Is it really safe?"

"By the way, she's left your rucksack."

"My rucksack?"

"There's also a box in the hall with your CDs…"

"My CDs…"

"Gram Parsons and the Flying Burrito Brothers."

"She hates Gram Parsons."

"There's also that DVD of yours. Highlights of the 1986 World Cup."

"Thank fuck for that. Where would I be without that?"

"Strangely, a copy of Somerset Maugham's The Moon and the Sixpence."

"That's for my soul."

"Shampoo, toothbrush… That girl thinks of everything", Graham said, shaking his head, as he sat down on the sofa. "Well, I suppose there is only one thing to do when you are given the sack."

Gavin brought out two beers from the fridge

"*Tutt' a post*," he said.

"*Tutt' a post*," said Graham and they settled down to watch the World Cup of Eighty-Six, even though they'd seen it a thousand and one times before

Sheep in the House

Brothers Nicola and Michele Campanile were neighbours of Guglielmo's cousin, Dino.

They lived down a woody dirt track several kilometers from the local town in a shared farmhouse. On one side of the house, Michele lived with his wife; Nicola lived on his own on the other side of the house.

Early one morning, when Nicola was already out on the tractor, Michele went next door to look for some coffee.

"*Non ci credo*. I don't believe it," he said, returning with coffee. "*C'è una pecora in casa*. He's got a sheep in the house."

Michele's wife put on the gas. "Well," she said, "I expect it's sick."

"Sick. *È mio fratello che è amalato.* My brother is the sick one."

When he came in from work, Michele made up his mind to speak to his brother. "Nicol'", he said, "what's all this business with the sheep?"

"*Niente,*" said his brother. "Nothing."

"What do you mean '*niente*'"?

"Mice', I'll be frank with you," he said. "She's come to live with me."

Michele went back inside and sat down.

His wife put the pasta on the table.

Michele did not say a word, as he tucked into the rigatoni with tomato sauce.

His wife looked across the table at him.

"What's the matter, Michele?"

"*Niente.*"

"What do you mean '*niente*'?"

"I'll be frank with you, wife," he said. "*La pecora dorme a casa di mio fratello.* The sheep has moved in next door."

Rosa Marina

The beach at Rosa Marina had always been a good spot for Daniel. Cabin cruisers and yachts of the new euro millionaires would come and weigh anchor in the bay. All of society seemed to gather here along the shore in the afternoon sun: the good-looking teenagers of the *alta borghese*, the Russians, Germans and Swedes on vacation, the dedicated followers of beach fashion and the bottomless sun-worshippers, hidden, along with the rest of the hoi polloi, among the narrow rocky places between the long stretches of golden sand.

Daniel was resting up with Ali about half way down the beach between the Grand Hotel and the end of the bay where he could see the pine trees of the camping site at Pineta. He had his clothes rail against the rocks. The rocks rose above his head forming a shadow along a narrow stretch of sand. Sometimes bathers would stop to admire his wares: the colourful beach dresses from India and African bubas and skirts, kaftans and khanga wraps. Daniel tried to hook them with a smile or a gestured greeting. Most would pass by without even looking his way. But Daniel was not offended. He behaved as if he was biding his time, watching them all with equanimity.

After a while, he picked up his bag and slung it over his shoulder. Dragging the clothes rail across the drying sand down by the shore, he turned and nodded to his friend, "*A dopo, bello.*"

There it was that he found her, a little way further down the beach from his resting place with Ali where the villas of the resort were a long way back from the dunes, and the sand itself was yellow and hot under foot.

A big, red parasol with Luna Rossa emblazoned over its red canopy had been hooked up for the benefit of a large man who was sitting in an upright navy deckchair, talking into his phone. There was a hamper and ice box with beers at his feet.

As Daniel approached, he became aware of the man's bulk, the folds of fat hanging impressively over his bathing shorts. For all that, he could see that the man had once been powerful and strong; his calves were still thick and muscular; all of which seemed to lend weight to the grave communion with the piece at his ear.

Sitting next to him, on an identical upright navy deck chair, was a middle-aged woman in a gold and black bikini, complemented by two large and clunky gold earrings. Her skin was a seasoned brown, but Daniel could see that she strove to look after herself with exercise and those occasional interventions that ladies of a certain age and class indulge in.

"*Buona sera*," he said, "can I interest you in my dresses? It is all *roba genuina* from Africa, Tibet, India. *Roba buona*. Good stuff."

"Giulia, are you coming to look?"

The Signora called over to a woman who was lying on the sand apart from her companions.

The woman looked up, squinting into the sun.

"Daniel," she said. "*Da quanto tempo!*"

"Julia," he said slowly as she got up and came towards him.

She smiled at him; Daniel smiled back.

"*Ti vedo bene,*" he said. "You look well."

"And you," she said. "How long has it been?"

"A long time…"

"Yes," she said, "it's been a long, long time."

"*Cosa sta succendo?*" he said. "What's happening here?"

"What does it look like?"

As she spoke, there was a familiar glint in her eye.

Daniel laughed.

"*Quant'è?*" the Signora called over to him. "How much is this?"

She was holding up one of his dresses, the one that was the colour of watermelon.

"Fifteen Euros."

"Fifteen," she said, raising an eyebrow. "It's too much. I'll give you ten."

Daniel turned back to Julia and smiled.

"The Signora is after a bargain."

"Patti, what have you got there?" said the man from the deckchair.

The Signora held up the watermelon dress.

"*Molto bello*! Giulia," he said, covering his phone with his hand, "you must buy something, too. This gentleman needs to make some money."

The man returned to his conversation.

"My husband has spoken," she said.

Daniel laughed.

"What about a khanga wrap?"

"You always did well with those."

He turned to the older woman.

"I give you special price, Signora. Ten Euros."

She went back to her chair and came back holding the note from her purse.

Daniel put it in the pouch around his middle.

"*Fa caldo*," she said. "It's hot."

"*Molto caldo*," said Daniel. "Very hot."

"*È molto carino il vestito.*"

"Thank you," he said in English.

The Signora smiled, returning to her chair under the parasol.

"What do you think?" said Julia, holding up a dress.

"Let me guess. She's your *suocera*[7]?"

---

[7] Mother-in-law.

Julia laughed.

"As a matter of fact, she is an old flame."

"In that case, you better watch out," he said. "These old flames don't settle for anything."

"You think she's still after him?"

Daniel smiled.

"Cofi ever tell you that story," he said, "the one about the djinn who bewitched a woman? The djinn turned her into a bird. When the husband returned to her, he found his wife old and ugly."

Julia laughed.

"How does it end?"

"They go on a journey. The bird follows. The djinn tells the husband to kill the bird so that she can have one of its feathers. The husband plucks the bird out of the sky. As he grasps the bird, the bird turns back into the man's wife."

"What happens to the djinn?"

"She disappears in a puff of smoke."

"Is that what is going to happen to her?"

"To be honest," said Daniel. "I have not yet worked out which one of you is the djinn."

Julia looked at him with smiling eyes.

"*Qu'est-ce que tu fais?*" she said. "What do you plan to do?"

Daniel shrugged.

"Head north."

"Perugia?"

He nodded and looked down the beach where the crowds were waiting for him. "*Bella*," he said eventually, "I better go now."

"Of course," she said. "How much do I owe you?"

"*Bella*, you don't owe me anything."

"Don't be silly. Achille," she said, turning and calling to the man on the deck chair, "have you got your wallet?"

She walked over and took the wallet from his hand and went back with it to Daniel.

The wallet was stuffed with notes.

"I'll take two of your khanga wraps," she said in a louder voice so the djinn and her husband might hear, "the yellow one and the red one."

She handed over the money. Daniel took it without looking at it and put it in his pouch.

He rummaged in his bag for the yellow and red khanga wraps.

"*Ci vediamo, bella.*"

"*Ci vediamo, bello.*"

She watched him go off, dragging the rail. Like some latter-day rag and bone man, Daniel disappeared into the crowds down the beach.

Julia turned and walked towards the shore when she heard a voice calling to her from the deckchair:

"Giulia, your back's going red. Don't you think you should come and sit under the parasol?"

"No, I don't think so," she said, smiling inwardly. "I'm going for a swim."

And she stepped out across the hot sand and walked down towards the water's edge.

Born in Poole, Dorset, in 1965, Sedley Proctor grew up in London and was educated in Winchester and Nottingham. He lived and worked as a teacher and translator in Southern Italy from the mid-nineties until 2013 when he returned to Britain. Apart from his own books, he writes under the aliases F.N. Frites and M.T. Sands.

ACKNOWLEDGEMENTS

The cover of this book has been designed with a derivative of an I-stock photo, woman on a beach, under a standard royalty free license. The Joker, or *Jolly Nero* has been derived from a digital photo donated by Trocche 100 to the public domain.

Accidental Death

Of a Terrorist

By Sedley Proctor

Crime passionnel in Southern Italy

What reasons can there be beyond the reasons of love?
Now married to successful businessman, Achille
Lombardo, Julia appears to have it all until her she
embarks on an ill-fated affair with Arturo, and her ex-pat
adventure morphs into the crime of passion.

Ten Naughty Stories

By M T Sands

"A luminous bit of prose delicately piled on prose platters"
Jay Parini

M.T. Sands grew up in southern England. She ran away from school when she was sixteen and lost her virtue in a field in Burgundy, under the vines of Clos de Tart, to a mystical and long-haired young German who claimed to be able to divine the kabbalah from a rather weathered notebook which had H. H. inscribed in fading, gold leaf on the cover. For several days she followed him on her bicycle until she ate some Pierre che Rire cheese and realized she was being an absolute fool. Thereafter her career began.

ALSO AVAILABLE FROM LEOPARD

CHILDREN'S FICTION

***

It was a matter of some urgency: a wolf was loose in the woods. And being loose in the woods, he could get into the garden.

"Whatever you do," said Dad. "Don't go out the gate. You don't want the wolf to eat you."

Laila went out the door, but the wolf was already in the garden.

"There you are!" he cried. "I was wondering where you got to."

"What are you doing here?" she cried. "This is my garden."

"Well," said the wolf, "you're not in your garden. You're in my garden now."

***

The Wolf Garden

By F. M. Frites

A Totally, Completely and Utterly Bodacious Adventure with Unicorns and Gnomes

Dreamy tomboy, Laila meets Cyril, a rebellious gnome and passes through a charmed gate into the Wolf Garden. Here, she does battle with the shape-shifter Smarm and his army of wolves. When Smarm captures her gnome friends and steals the magic strawbs, Laila and Cyril help the Mistress Dido win them back.

www.ingramcontent.com/pod-product-compliance
Lightning Source LLC
Chambersburg PA
CBHW021034130626
46552CB00005B/1838